The
Rising Star
of
Rusty Nail

The
Rising Star
of
Rusty Nail

Lesley M. M. Blume

Alfred A. Knopf   New York

THIS IS A BORZOI BOOK PUBLISHED BY ALFRED A. KNOPF

Published in the United States by Alfred A. Knopf, an imprint of Random House Children's Books, a division of Random House, Inc., New York.

KNOPF, BORZOI BOOKS, and the colophon are registered trademarks of Random House, Inc.

www.randomhouse.com/kids

Educators and librarians, for a variety of teaching tools, visit us at www.randomhouse.com/teachers

Library of Congress Cataloging-in-Publication Data
Blume, Lesley M. M.
The rising star of Rusty Nail / Lesley M. M. Blume. — 1st ed.
  p. cm.
SUMMARY: In the small town of Rusty Nail, Minnesota, in the early 1950s, musically talented, ten-year-old Franny wants to take advanced piano lessons from newcomer Olga Malenkov, a famous Russian musician suspected of being a communist spy by gossipy members of the community.
ISBN 978-0-375-83524-7 (trade) — ISBN 978-0-375-93524-4 (lib. bdg.)
[1. Piano—Fiction. 2. Musicians—Fiction. 3. Russian Americans—Fiction.
4. Country life—Minnesota—Fiction. 5. Minnesota—History—20th century—Fiction.] I. Title.
PZ7.B62567Ri 2007
[Fic]—dc22
2006024252

Printed in the United States of America

June 2007

10 9 8 7 6 5 4 3 2

First Edition

To the *real* star of Rusty Nail;

she knows who she is.

The
Rising Star
of
Rusty Nail

The structure of this book is modeled on that of Russian composer Sergei Rachmaninoff's Piano Concerto no. 2, op. 18, which is considered by many to be one of the greatest piano concertos of all time.

By definition, a concerto is "a composition with three movements, in which one instrument stands out against the orchestra to display the performer's musical skill."

In other words, there can only be one star in a concerto. Not two or three—just one.

Part One of this book, like the first movement of Rachmaninoff's concerto, is called "Moderato." It is fast and spirited, and sets the stage for what's to come.

Part Two, "Adagio," is named for the concerto's second movement. In it, tension slowly builds, leading up to big excitement in the third movement.

And finally, Part Three is called "Allegro." Swift and riveting, it is the dramatic culmination of the entire performance.

Part I

Moderato

Chapter One

"Franny, you throw like a *girl,*" said Sandy with disgust as she expertly tied the end of a water-filled balloon into a knot.

"I do *not,*" scowled Franny. "I got Rodney the jail janitor right on the back of the head, and you haven't even hit a single person."

"Oh yes, I did. I pegged ole Norma Smitty when you ran downstairs to get more water."

"Really?" said Franny suspiciously. "I didn't hear her yelling or anything."

"Oh, she yelled all right," boasted Sandy, tossing her balloon onto a gurgling pile of water bombs. "She said, 'Sandy Anne Hellickson and Frances Hansen—I know that's you up there! You ain't foolin' me! When I tell yer fathers that you was throwin' water bombs off the top of that buildin', yer gonna be sorry you was ever born!'"

The girls doubled up with laughter. They were stationed on the top of the two-story building on Main Street where Franny lived with her parents and two older brothers. With its wooden false front jutting five feet above the roof, the building was practically a skyscraper in their tiny town—if Rusty Nail, Minnesota, could really be described as a "town" at all. In reality, it was little more than a bunch of dusty houses and stores clumped together in the middle of nowhere. For miles and miles, a seemingly endless carpet of cornfields surrounded the community. Cows and rust-colored barns dotted the countryside, and tractors drove slowly along the dirt roads.

Long ago, Rusty Nail had been a pioneer outpost. But when the winters proved too harsh for the settlers, they took apart their makeshift wooden houses and piled the planks into their creaky covered wagons. No one knows where they went next, and the only thing they left behind was a pile of old bent nails. The next homesteaders who plunked along and settled in the area found these artifacts, and dutifully named the town Rusty Nail in 1879.

These days, in 1953, Rusty Nail's countryside was inhabited by weatherworn farmers, with a few store owners and regular folks mixed in. In the middle of the town square stood a sign, dulled by years of exposure to fierce summer thunderstorms and howling winter blizzards. It proclaimed:

WELCOME TO RUSTY NAIL!
FORMERLY THE AMERICAN COOT CAPITAL OF THE WORLD!

The American coot was a bird that looked sort of like a duck. Like the pioneers, one year they'd decided to just up and leave. Rumor had it that they found Iowa more to their liking, and as a result, Rusty Nail was left with only the fond memory of the Era of the Coot.

The sleepy town had only one of everything: one grocery store, one church, one lawyer, one doctor, one bar, even one old drunk who shambled aimlessly around the town square. There was even only one stoplight, which hung desolately on a thick wire over the intersection of Main Street and Church Street. Sometimes the light worked, and sometimes it didn't. But in any case, most of the townspeople drove their rusted Ford pickup trucks so slowly that it didn't matter one way or another.

Time dragged in Rusty Nail and nothing ever seemed to happen. Even the flies in the air seemed to stand still, as though suspended inside honey-colored amber. The slow passing of time showed itself by the rising and falling of the sun, the changing of the seasons, and children growing up and then growing old and replacing themselves with a new generation of children to grow up and grow old in Rusty Nail.

But most of the time, this didn't bother Franny and Sandy. To them, Rusty Nail was the center of the universe. They had been lifelong best friends, for ten whole years.

Sandy was the undisputed ringleader, even though she was several months younger than Franny.

On this day, the last of summer vacation, Franny and Sandy were playing their favorite game: "Invasion of the Commies," as Russians were popularly known in those days. Inspired by a war movie the girls had seen at the rather shoddy Hauser's Movie Palace at the end of Main Street, the game involved throwing water balloons at people on the street below, pretending that they were looting-and-pillaging Russian soldiers. Franny and Sandy, of course, pretended to be American soldiers defending their hometown.

Only the day before, Sandy had received an extra-large mail shipment of water balloons from the Finkelstein Prank & Curiosity Company of Cedar Rapids, Iowa. This meant that the game could last until well after sunset—provided, of course, that they didn't get caught.

Sandy stood on a rickety metal stool, poked her head over the top of the false front, and surveyed the street below. A few farmers in dirty denim overalls lumped up the sidewalk and disappeared into the Arflot Saddle and Harness Store. The shredded, dirty screen door to Elmer's Bar slapped open, and Old Bill Codger shuffled out, scratching his rear end and blinking dimly in the late-afternoon sun.

Suddenly something caught Sandy's attention.

"Oh, goody," she said excitedly. "Stella's on her way up the sidewalk! Quick, pass me that balloon—I mean, that grenade."

She shoved a handful of cinnamon Red Hots into her mouth as Franny scrambled over with a water bomb. Stella Brunsvold owned the old-fashioned popcorn stand in front of Hauser's. A mean old gossip, she spent her time spitting out corn kernels at children and chasing them away from the theater.

"Here's the grenade, Lieutenant!" shouted Franny. "Let 'er rip!"

"Take that, Comrade!" Sandy yelled with glee as she tossed the balloon over the edge of the building. *Comrade,* according to the movies, was what Russians called each other. A few seconds later, the girls heard a satisfying *splat!* followed by a loud squawk.

"Quick—look and see if you hit her," said Franny urgently.

"Dang," Sandy said, peeking over the false front. "I missed Comrade Stella—but I did get the Snurrs." An ancient pair of spinsters who ran the five-and-dime store, the Snurr sisters still wore long black pioneer dresses that covered their wrists and ankles.

"They don't count," Franny scoffed. "They walk so slowly that a blind man could hit them."

"Fine, if you're such a good shot, then *you* hit Comrade Stella," said Sandy, tossing Franny a balloon. "Hey, Franny."

"What?"

"This is a lot more fun than practicin' the piano all day, huh?"

Franny paused. "Sure," she said, since that was clearly what Sandy wanted to hear.

"Boy," said Sandy, eating more candy. Her lips and tongue were turning fiery red. "I'd go crazy for sure if I practiced as much as you do. You're lucky you still got any fingers left."

"Go on and laugh," said Franny, a little embarrassed by Sandy's teasing, because there was more than a kernel of truth in it. Indeed, she was a good pianist—a far better one than anyone would ever expect to find in a place like Rusty Nail. And she *did* spend a lot of time practicing at the old upright piano in her family's living room. She went on: "Laugh good and hard, but I have a plan, you know."

"What kind of plan?"

"Well," Franny said, juggling the plump balloon in her hands. "If the Commies came for real, I'd save my family with our piano."

Sandy looked skeptical. "How'd you do that? By pushin' it off the roof on top of the Russians?"

"No-o," Franny said, annoyed. "I'd *play* it. The Commies would bust into the town and go door-to-door with their guns, just like in the movies. They'd round everyone up and send them over to the square. But when they got to *my* apartment, I'd be ready. When they kicked down the front door—there I'd be, sitting at the piano. And I'd start playing some Tchaikovsky."

"What's that—some kinda hypnotist song?" Sandy asked.

"No, dummy—Tchaikovsky is a Russian composer," answered Franny. "And when the soldiers heard me play Russian music, they'd be so moved to hear it, so far away from home, that they'd spare me and my family. That's why I have to practice all the time."

"That's the stupidest thing I've ever heard," said Sandy. "I'd just work on your aim if I were you. And if you don't hurry up, Comrade Stella's gonna get away."

Franny helped herself to some of Sandy's Red Hots, stood up on the stool behind the false front, and looked down at the sidewalk. The damp Snurrs still stood there, squinting in confusion at the sky, as though expecting it to rain doughnuts next. Stella prowled around the building like a hungry alley cat, looking for the culprits who'd drenched the ancient sisters. Then a new person came into view, and Franny's heart pounded with wild excitement.

It was the girls' classmate and official Number One Class-A Enemy: Nancy Orilee.

She was, without a doubt, an infinitely hateable creature. Her father owned a seed plant and was the richest man in Rusty Nail, and her mother had won second place in a beauty contest at a dairy fair once. In addition, Nancy got straight As and was always the teacher's pet. *And,* to top it all off, her father paid a special piano teacher to drive from a town forty miles away to give Nancy a weekly lesson.

Franny, on the other hand, was far from perfect.

Schoolwork bored her. Her family struggled to make ends meet, and no beauty awards hung on the Hansens' living-room walls.

In short, Franny simply could not compete with Nancy Orilee—*except* when it came to playing the piano. In fact, music was the one area in which Franny might have been even *better* than her rival. And, of course, this made Nancy hate Franny, for the Orilees were famous for detesting anything that resembled healthy competition. Sandy, on the other hand, couldn't keep up with Nancy in *any* department, and had to settle for loathing her from the sidelines.

Needless to say, Franny and Sandy were thrilled to see Nancy trotting up Main Street.

"Lieutenant!" Franny yelled to Sandy. "It's the big one—the one we've all been waiting for! Comrade *Orilee* at three o'clock!"

She hastily pitched her balloon over the side of the building, and Sandy, squealing with glee, threw an extra bomb for good measure. They hunkered down and waited for Nancy's shriek.

Instead, to their horror, they heard the sound of squealing tires, a blaring car horn, and a crash, followed by a chorus of shrieking chickens. A flurry of feathers swirled up into the air.

Sandy's face went white. "What in Sam Hill?" she said as she leaped up on the stool and looked down at the street below.

"Oh boy—are we gonna get it," she said in a shaky voice as she sank down behind the false front.

"What happened?" Franny gasped.

"One of the balloons hit Mayor Reverend Jerry's windshield, and he ran his car right into Mr. Klompenhower's chicken cart!" Sandy exclaimed. The Red Hots fell right out of Franny's mouth. "And of course, it all has to happen in front of Prancy Orilee—it's just not *fair*! Oh boy, oh boy—are we goners. Quick—we gotta hide these balloons! Stamp on 'em!"

The girls threw all of the balloons onto the rooftop and leaped up and down on them. One after another, the water bombs exploded until the girls were soaking wet. They were snatching up the scraps of rubber when loud footsteps pounded up the stairs to the roof. The metal roof door banged open. In the doorway towered Franny's father, Wes Hansen, whose accounting office occupied the first floor of the building.

Sandy stood there, a dripping balloon wrapped around her shoe. "Hi, Mr. Hansen," she said as sunnily as possible. "What brings you up this way?"

Looking like he'd just been shot out of a geyser, Wes stormed onto the roof.

"Fran-*ces*," he said in his most terrible voice. "You are grounded for the rest of your life. Downstairs—*now*. Both of you."

And that was how Franny and Sandy ended their summer vacation.

Later that evening, Franny lay like a board on her bed in the family's second-floor apartment, awaiting her doom. Of course, she'd been sent to her room without supper (which, in the Hansen house, wasn't necessarily a punishment since Franny's mother, Lorraine, was a famously awful chef). Still, her stomach grumbled as she heard the clink of the silverware against the plates from the kitchen mixing with the murmur of *The Bob Hope Show* coming from the big, clunky radio in the living room.

"I swear, Lorraine," Franny heard her father say to her mother, "I'm lucky that I still have teeth after sixteen years of your cooking. You could pave a road with this meatloaf." Franny's older brothers, Owen and Jessie, snickered.

Franny's mother giggled. "Oh, it won't kill you, Wes," she said. "And if it's really that bad, you know where to find the apron and the pans."

The boys laughed again. Owen was fifteen and Jessie fourteen, and they'd eat anything put down in front of them.

Wes sighed. "Just give me some coffee, please. I don't have the energy to saw this into little pieces anymore."

Franny's stomach flip-flopped when she heard this. She knew that once Wes finished his coffee, he'd come down the hallway to give her the Talking-To-Of-All-Talking-To's. Five minutes later, when he opened her bedroom door, Franny squeezed her eyes shut and pretended to be asleep.

"Cut it out, Franny," Wes said. "That's the oldest trick in the book."

Franny sat up straight as an arrow and blurted out the first thing that came to her mind: "Sandy made me do it."

Wes pulled a chair out from under her wooden desk and sat down.

"You're just lucky that you and Sandy aren't spending the night in jail—do you know that?"

Franny nodded glumly.

"You girls are going to earn back the money that it costs to repair the mayor's car and Mr. Klompenhower's chicken cart. I don't care if it takes months of odd jobs during the afternoons and weekends. And then I want you to write a note of apology to every person that you hit. And that includes Nancy Orilee, since I assume that you *intended* to hit her with that last balloon."

This was simply too much. "Da-a-a-d!" Franny wailed. "Please don't make me! She'll never let me forget it!"

Wes gave her a stern look. "Franny—I know that you've disliked Nancy since you were little girls, but you're getting far too old for these kinds of shenanigans. Let me tell you this: you might think that it'll put Nancy in her place if you hit her with a water balloon—but in reality, it only makes you look like a hooligan." He sighed. "I want you to start letting everyone in Rusty Nail know that you're someone special—a fine, talented pianist—not a little roughneck."

"How come no one ever tells Sandy to be special?"

Franny asked grumpily. Sometimes she hated that word, since it set her apart so starkly from everyone else her age, like having a clubfoot or an extra finger. "Or Owen, or Jessie?"

Her father frowned at her. "Because you're different from them, whether you like it or not. You've got a gift and a chance that very few people have, and they don't. It could be your ticket to the top, you know. *I* had a chance to be a big-deal musician once—did you know that? Did I ever tell you about the time Duke Ellington came to town?"

"Only about a thousand times," groaned Franny. Long ago, Wes had played the trumpet, but these days he rarely took it out of its case. The brass instrument lay silently smothered in the black-velvet lining of the coffin-like case. But even though he didn't play anymore, he still liked to regale *everyone* in Rusty Nail with his Duke Ellington story several times a year.

"I was eighteen years old," Wes continued, as though he hadn't heard Franny at all. "I spent all of my days working on your grandpa's farm and my evenings studying to become an accountant. And then, late at night, I'd take my trumpet out into the cornfields, so no one could hear me, and practice under the moon, sometimes till dawn. By God, did I get good! And guess what happened then?"

"The legendary Duke Ellington and his big, famous swing band drove into Rusty Nail during one of their small-town tours and gave a big concert at the school gym," Franny recited automatically. "And you brought your trumpet in and played for him, and he asked you to join the band and travel all over the world, but you couldn't go because you were already engaged to Mom."

Wes rubbed his jaw and stared at the bedroom wall.

"Now, *that* was an exciting night," he said, clearly in another world. "You should have seen it. That man rolled into town with three buses of instruments and musicians, and people drove in from all over the countryside. And Duke and his boys played hard into the wee hours, and folks were dancing like it was their last night on earth. It was hot as blazes in that room, and then I got up on the stage with my trumpet and . . ."

He stopped, lost in his favorite memory. Then his smile faded and he looked down at his daughter.

"Well, anyway," he said, clearing his throat. "What I'm saying is that if you keep behaving like a hoodlum and squandering your opportunities, you'll be the main person to regret it. At some point down the line, you won't want to settle for just being average—but by then it will be too late. Take it from me." He was silent for a moment, and then added: "Now write your letters and go to bed. I don't want to see you again till the morning."

And he left the room, closing the door behind him.

Franny got out of bed and gloomily sat down at her desk and watched the sky turn violet and then black as the sun set. The smells of cooling tar from the street below and sweet hay from the fields mixed in the breeze and filled her bedroom. The town's sole stoplight swung lazily on its wire, dutifully clicking as it changed from red to green to yellow and back to red again.

The colors reflected on Franny's face as she sharpened some pencils. She scowled as she wrote her note to Nancy:

Dear Nancy,
My dad's making me say I'm sorry that me and Sandy threw a water balloon at you.
Sincerely,
Frances Hansen

She thought about spitting on the note as she folded it up, but decided that she was already in too much trouble to risk it.

Chapter Two

The next morning after breakfast, Franny met Sandy outside the James K. Polk School, where they had gone since kindergarten. Rusty Nail was so small that the elementary school, junior high, and high school were all part of the same brick building.

Sandy sulkily parked her bike at the school rack. Her family lived on a big farm outside the town, and she bicycled two miles to school every morning and back again in the afternoons, braving all sorts of weather.

"Daddy says that I'm grounded forever," she complained.

"Me too," said Franny. "I had to write six apology notes last night—even to the people that *you* hit. And the worst part is that my dad told me that I had to write one to . . . Nancy."

Sandy gasped. "No! Not to *Prancy*! Did you do it?"

"I *had* to," Franny said, showing Sandy the note. The girls read it together and then stared at each other in despair.

"Yeah, well—guess what," Sandy said grimly. "It gets even worse. We already have our first job. My dad talked to Mr. Klompenhower last night. He says that he'll let us off the hook about the chicken cart if we fix a big hole in his pig barn. Crazy Frankie drove his car into the barn last week." Crazy Frankie was Mr. Klompenhower's no-good son, who went on what Franny's father called "benders."

"Wow," said Franny. "Mr. Klompenhower sure has bad luck these days."

"No, *we* have bad luck," said Sandy. "A *pig* barn. Do you even *know* how bad those things smell?"

The girls stopped to consider this. Franny already felt nauseated.

"And on top of everything else," Sandy added, "Daddy took away all my candy."

Franny secretly thought that this was probably a good thing, since Sandy already had a vast array of cavities and fillings in her teeth from eating Red Hots all the time.

"How long do you think Miss Hamm will last this year?" Franny asked, changing the subject to a happier topic. "I give her two weeks."

Last year, Miss Hamm, Rusty Nail's young fifth-grade

teacher, had had a nervous breakdown right in the middle of a standard duck-and-cover drill. These were like fire drills, but instead of leaving the building, all of the kids were supposed to crawl under their desks and put their hands over the backs of their heads. This was supposed to protect them in case the Commies ever lobbed a nuclear bomb in the direction of Rusty Nail.

"Ha! I give her two days, tops," Sandy said, her mood brightening somewhat. "Come on, let's go grab desks next to each other."

They were walking up the school's front stairs when a voice behind them said: "What nice overalls you're wearing, Sandy Anne! They make it harder than ever to tell that you're a girl."

Franny and Sandy spun around and saw Nancy Orilee smirking at them.

"That's a nice face you've got there, Prancy," Sandy retorted. "Were all of the piggies in your litter as good-looking as you?"

Nancy's smile hardened a little. "Ha ha," she said. "*You're* the one who lives in a barn, not me. By the way, that was a nice stunt you pulled yesterday. I was *so* glad that I was there to see it. My father says that you'll both end up in jail."

Franny wished that she had one of their water balloons at that exact moment. But instead, with enormous effort, she extended her hand with the apology note toward Nancy.

Nancy took a step back. "What's that?" she asked suspiciously.

"Just some dumb note my dad made me write," Franny mumbled, wishing that she could shrink down to the size of a bug and scuttle away. She would *never* forgive her father for putting her through this.

Nancy snatched it up and read it. A huge, gloating grin spread across her face.

"You shouldn't have even bothered," she said, crumpling up the note and dropping it on the ground. "Your handwriting's so bad that I couldn't even read it." And she sailed past the girls with her nose in the air.

"If I wasn't already in so much trouble, I would've slugged her right in the nose," Sandy said.

"We'll get back at her later," Franny said miserably. She pulled out a packet of Beemans gum and handed Sandy a piece as they walked into the school.

Wonderful chaos reigned in the fifth-grade classroom since Miss Hamm had yet to arrive. Several boys stood on their desks, throwing paper airplanes and pencils at each other. Runty Knutson, the class troublemaker and one of Sandy's favorite cohorts, scratched dirty words on the chalkboard with a piece of blue chalk. Gretchen Beasley, the class crybaby, was already sniveling. Sandy and Franny smiled slyly at each other. It was good to be back.

Presently, Miss Hamm inched into the room. Pitifully skinny and parched-looking, she reminded Franny of a dry twig. Her flowered dress hung limply on her bony frame, and even the pink carnation she'd pinned to her breast had sadly wilted. Everyone in the class froze and gaped at her. She stood at the front of the room and let out a squeaky little noise.

"Whaddya say?" said Runty rudely.

"Oh!" yelped Miss Hamm. Steadying herself on her big oak desk, she said: "I said, please take your seats, children." Then she saw the curse words covering the board. *"Oh!"* she said again helplessly, and vigorously erased them, sending chalk dust flying everywhere.

Meanwhile, all of the kids went into a mad scramble for the desks they wanted. Sandy and Franny miraculously got seats right behind Nancy, which meant they could throw spitballs at her blond head all year.

"All right, class," said Miss Hamm weakly. "Why don't we go around the room so each of you can stand up and say a few words about how you spent the summer?"

Franny sighed. Her teachers started every school year with the same exercise, and Franny never thought that her stories sounded exciting enough. She'd spent most of this past summer out at the Hellicksons' farm, wading with Sandy in the murky frog pond or playing hide-and-seek in the cornfield. And of course, taking piano lessons at the mildewy home of her music teacher, the dreary Mrs. Staudt. She sank down low in her seat and hoped that Miss Hamm would skip her.

Runty stood up first and proudly announced that he'd spent the summer building slop troughs at his father's pig farm. Sandy went next, and she made up a fabulous story about traveling with the circus and running the freak-show tent.

"We had to feed the bearded Siamese-twin ladies raw steaks every morning, or they'd eat one of the kids in the audience," she declared.

"Oh my," said Miss Hamm, wringing her hands.

Then it was Nancy Orilee's turn. "My daddy bought the first TV in Rusty Nail and set it up in our living room," she bragged. "It cost five hundred dollars and we get two whole channels. We set up three rows of folding chairs in front of it like a movie theater, and invited everybody in the neighborhood to come over and watch *The Roy Rogers Show*. Well, almost everyone."

And with that comment, she looked straight at Franny and Sandy, who, of course, had received no such invitation. Nancy smiled meanly and went on: "And then Daddy sent me to a special music camp, where I took piano lessons with very important teachers who told me that I'm the best young pianist in all of Minnesota, and probably Iowa too." Then she looked around the room again, as if expecting applause, and then sat down like a queen settling into her throne.

"Oh, brother," said Sandy under her breath. She scribbled something on a piece of paper, folded it up, and discreetly passed it to Franny. It said:

Franny took her gum out of her mouth and handed it to Sandy, who added it to her own gob. When Miss Hamm faced the blackboard, Sandy planted the gooey wad right smack into Nancy's hair.

Miss Hamm nearly hit the ceiling when she heard Nancy's shriek.

"God almighty!" she cried, gripping her throat with her hand. "What's happening?"

Nancy tugged at her hair hysterically. "Miss Hamm! Miss Hamm! Sandy Anne put *gum* in my hair!" she shrieked.

Just then, the principal, Mr. Moody, stomped into the room. No one could ever figure out why he worked in a school, since he hated kids almost as much as Stella Brunsvold, the popcorn lady, did. Brown stains spattered his necktie, as though someone had blown coffee at him through a drinking straw, and a wet blue inkblot adorned his front shirt pocket.

"Quiet!" he bellowed. "What's going on here?"

Trembling like a witness in a murder trial, Miss Hamm explained.

Mr. Moody sighed irritably. "Nancy, go to the nurse and have her deal with the gum. Sandy Anne, go to my office—you know the way well."

This was true—every year, Sandy practically made a rut in the floor from her desk to the principal's office. Nancy stamped out of the room. Sandy trudged out after her.

"Now then," said Mr. Moody. "Listen to me—each and every one of you little savages. If you give Miss Hamm any more trouble, you'll spend the year studying in my office. Think about it."

A chill of horror went through the classroom. The idea of spending even a minute in Mr. Moody's office was too awful to think about. Firstly, he smoked so much that no one could even see across the room, and secondly, everyone knew that he spent the whole day coughing and loudly clipping his yellow fingernails into a wastebasket under his desk.

"I'm glad that we understand each other," Mr. Moody continued darkly. "Welcome back to the James K. Polk School. The mayor has just informed me that Rusty Nail is going to have a very important visitor soon. Furthermore, we're going to have a school assembly in honor of the guest. And I will not tolerate gum infractions, name-calling, spitball throwing, hair yanking, yelling, hollering, hooting, whining, profanity, seat kicking, outbursts, horsing around, note passing, booby traps, trick playing, or any other bad behavior. Understood?"

All of the students nodded grudgingly, except for Runty, who belched under his breath.

"Oh yes, Mr. Moody, we understand," Miss Hamm breathed.

Mr. Moody looked disgusted. "Get ahold of yourself, woman," he said, and clomped out of the room. Miss

Hamm smiled feebly at her students as she began handing out arithmetic books.

It's going to be a long year, Franny thought.

At recess, the schoolyard buzzed with speculation about who the mystery visitor would be. Why would *anyone* want to come to Rusty Nail? Besides the wild visit of Duke Ellington sixteen years earlier, the last time someone famous had come was when the state governor ended up there courtesy of a highway car accident. He fled again as quickly as possible, but not before getting food poisoning at a church meatball supper hastily assembled in his honor.

"I hope it's John Wayne," said Runty. "I want him to teach me how to ride backward on a horse." John Wayne was a famous movie star who always played cowboy parts.

"Aw, John Wayne's a sissy," scoffed Harold Hrapp, who was skinny as a chicken bone. "Gene Autry—now, *that's* a real cowboy. He can clean up ten Injuns with a single bullet. I hope it's him that's comin'." And with that, he kicked up some dust onto Runty's feet.

Thora Vilborg pushed her smudgy glasses up on her nose. "Who wants a stinky old cowboy to come here?" she said. "I want it to be Jane Russell—I've seen her in eight movies down at Hauser's."

All of the girls began arguing over whether Jane Russell

or Ava Gardner was the bigger movie star while Runty and Harold continued kicking dirt at each other.

Soon Sandy and Nancy Orilee came out of the building and joined the group. The school nurse had massaged peanut butter into Nancy's hair until the gum slid out, and now her hair had been raked back into a greasy ponytail. Sandy smelled as though she'd spent the morning emptying ashtrays in Elmer's Bar on Main Street. Apparently, Mr. Moody's office was as smoke filled as ever.

"What happened?" Franny immediately asked Sandy.

"Nothing, really," Sandy replied. "I mean, he called my mom, but what are they gonna do? I'm already grounded for life—are they gonna ground me when I'm dead too?"

When she learned about the mystery person due to arrive in Rusty Nail, she immediately voted for Willie Mays, the baseball player. "So he can teach me how to throw like a champ," she said. "I wanna be the first girl to play in the major leagues. Hey, Franny—who do you hope it is?"

Franny tried to remember the names of all of the movie stars she'd seen in films down at Hauser's, but the only thing that came to mind was the string of Westerns and outer-space movies she and Sandy had seen the week before.

But then she remembered something else.

They had been sitting there, last Friday, watching the newsreel that came before that evening's feature film, *Goldtown Ghost Riders*. Usually the newsreels bored Franny and

Sandy since all of the stories featured a senator named so-and-so McCarthy, who always harped on and on about the so-called Commie Menace. According to him, secret agents were determined to turn regular folks into Commies and bring America down from the inside.

But on this particular day, part of the newsreel was about a girl from New York—only nine years old—who had been invited to give a piano concert for President Eisenhower and his wife at the White House. Franny had sat up straight in her creaking seat. Her heart pounded and her fingers tensed as she watched the girl play and then bow to the president and first lady. *Why aren't I the one up on that stage?* Franny had thought. *That girl's a whole year younger than me!* She sulked jealously for the rest of the afternoon.

And now, in the schoolyard, Franny found herself wishing that Rusty Nail's famous visitor would be someone who could help her, somehow, get onto a stage like that uppity nine-year-old. Some sort of Hollywood agent would be best, she supposed, but that would probably be way too much to hope for. *Maybe if the governor comes back,* she thought rapidly, *and somehow he hears me play, he'll go to Washington and tell the president about me, and I'll get an invitation to play at the White House too. Or maybe—*

Franny suddenly realized that the other kids were staring at her, and her face reddened.

"I hope it's Willie Mays too," she said quickly, mostly to show solidarity with Sandy.

This brought the discussion to an end, and the class played kickball on the dry, patchy lawn until the bell rang.

When the bell rang at three o'clock, Franny watched with envy as her classmates ran off to buy baseball cards and candy cigarettes and wax lips at the Snurr sisters' five-and-dime store. Then she walked resentfully over to Mrs. Staudt's house, clutching her music books. It was time for her weekly piano lesson.

Franny might have been smart-alecky to her father about her talent, but the plain truth was that she loved playing the piano. She also loved being good at playing the piano, which isn't necessarily the same thing. Furthermore, she loved it that people *knew* that she was a good pianist, which is a different thing altogether.

But she detested her actual lessons—and hated knowing that everyone else was off having a grand old time while she was a prisoner in Mrs. Staudt's stuffy music room.

Mrs. Staudt lived in a rickety old house with her ancient father, who "didn't have all of his marbles anymore," as Franny's mother put it. Usually he had been stashed away in a room upstairs when Franny arrived for her lesson, but sometimes he would escape and wander into the music room. This was always very exciting because the old man usually had some interesting things to say for himself.

Franny walked up the splintery front stairs and rang the doorbell.

Eventually the plump Mrs. Staudt materialized, a cigarette hanging sullenly from her lower lip. Rhinestones glinted around the edges of her black horn-rimmed spectacles, lending a hint of vitality to Mrs. Staudt's otherwise lusterless presence.

"All right, girlie," she rasped. "Into the music room with you."

Franny strolled into the next room and plopped herself down on the piano bench.

"What was your assignment again?" Mrs. Staudt asked disinterestedly as she arranged her bulk in a chair near the piano.

"Bach," Franny replied glibly. They had worked on the same Bach piece for four weeks in a row—but Mrs. Staudt never remembered this. In fact, Sandy and Franny had a running bet on how long Franny could get away with playing the same thing over and over again in her lesson.

Mrs. Staudt just nodded and took a long drag on the cigarette.

"Go on, then, girlie," she said, and yawned.

Franny began to play. Today, instead of being amused about getting away with the old Bach ploy, she was annoyed. How was she ever going to get good enough to play on stage with such an old fool of a teacher? Once in a while, she glanced resentfully over at Mrs. Staudt. Halfway through the music piece, Franny noticed with astonishment that her teacher appeared to be nodding off to sleep, her smoldering cigarette still dangling from her mouth. Franny added a few wrong notes here and there to see if the teacher would notice, but Mrs. Staudt showed no signs of life.

At the end of the piece, Franny played as loud as she could without hurting herself, thundering to a deafening finale. Mrs. Staudt rewarded her student with a grunty little snore.

Franny stared at her teacher in disbelief. After a minute, she slammed down the heavy keyboard lid with a loud bang.

Mrs. Staudt shot up in her seat as though someone had stuck her with a red-hot branding iron. Her cigarette fell in her lap, and she slapped at the burning ashes. Then she smacked her lips several times and said groggily: "Very good, girlie. You've been practicing."

Franny could hardly believe her own ears.

"Why don't you run through it again, so I can watch your finger work," suggested Mrs. Staudt, looking ready for another little nap.

Suddenly the door to the music room swung open. Franny felt a surge of glee when she heard the labored breathing coming from the hallway. Then Mrs. Staudt's father staggered in, looking panicked and disheveled. He wore a ratty old bathrobe and fluffy pink slippers with felt bunny ears sticking out of them.

"Who got shot?" he wheezed, leaning on his cane. "I

heard a shot! Who got the gun out? The Commies are comin', ain't they? I tole ya and tole ya, but y'never listen t' me!"

"Da-a-ad!" Mrs. Staudt shouted. "It was just the keyboard lid on the piano. Get back up those stairs!" She lurched out of her chair, which emitted a grateful groan.

Then the old man fixed his beady old eyes on Franny and sharply drew in his breath.

"Well, as I live and breathe," he gasped, staring at Franny as though she was his long-lost child. He tottered toward her urgently and exclaimed: "Mr. President— you're here just in the nick of time. Things're real bad here in Rusty Nail, Mr. President—oh, you betcha! All the hogs got the fever!"

That was as much as he managed to get out before Mrs. Staudt turned him around and marched him to the door.

"Upstairs—now!" she yelled as she shoveled him along. One of his bunny slippers fell off and lay forlornly on the floor.

Her father called desperately over his shoulder to Franny: "We need more farm subsidies, Mr. President!" and then he disappeared through the door.

Franny sat there on the piano bench and scowled. She was sure that Tchaikovsky or Nancy or even that dumb nine-year-old girl at the White House never had to tolerate such indignities at a piano lesson.

A few minutes later, Mrs. Staudt plodded back into the

room. She didn't even mention the incident but just threw herself down into her chair and lit another cigarette.

"Now then, where were we?" she asked pleasantly, ashes falling on her large bosom.

Franny played the Bach piece for her teacher three more times and trudged home, heavyhearted.

Chapter Three

Mayor Reverend Jerry was in a pickle. He sat in a fuchsia-colored vinyl chair at the local beauty salon, chomping on the damp end of an unlit cigar and thinking hard. All of the men in Rusty Nail had to go to the Smitty Beauty Station since the town barbershop had closed unexpectedly three years earlier. The owner of the barbershop, Mr. Rudolph Buck, had gone to Las Vegas for a vacation, fallen in love with a showgirl named Luella, and simply never come back.

The mayor, also the town's only minister, had just strolled into the Smitty salon for a haircut. Since the owner, Miss Norma Smitty, had already gone home for the night, the only person left to tend to him was the slothful salon assistant, Melba. The mayor's heart sank since Melba was a terrible beautician who could do only two things: provide a permanent wave and cut a bowl haircut. In the latter procedure, Melba would literally slap a plastic bowl over the customer's head and cut around the edges of it, leaving a perfectly round, mushroom-like cap on top of the customer's head.

Under normal circumstances, Mayor Reverend Jerry would have fretted over the unsavory options—but today he had bigger problems.

"All right, Melba," he said. "I need you to neaten up my appearance. It's gonna be a busy week, and I ain't gonna have time for any grooming. So let's get it right the first time."

Melba reluctantly put down her magazine, a tattered copy of *Silver Screen*.

"What'll it be, then, Mayor Reverend," Melba asked. "You know the choices."

The mayor mused over this for a minute, and then said: "Whatever looks more citified, I guess. We've got a real important guest comin' to town, and I wanna make a good impression."

"Wel-l-l," Melba said, pondering the possibilities. "All them movie stars have kinda wavy hair these days. We can stick some curlers in yers and then grease it back a little, like Tony Curtis or Desi Arnaz."

The mayor agreed. Melba drew the curtains shut in the front windows and put curlers and permanent-wave solution all over the mayor's head. Then there was nothing to do but stare at each other while the perm settled in. Melba soon tired of this and buried her snout in her magazine again, and the mayor began chomping on his cigar again anxiously.

A few minutes passed, and then Melba broke the silence. "Why on earth are you always chewin' on that thing?" she asked the mayor, irritated by all of his smacking and gnashing. "You don' even bother to light it."

"My wife won't let me have cigars anymore," he said woefully. "But I guess she can't fault me if I chew on it without smokin' it. Now put that magazine down, Melba. I got a real problem and I want your opinion on it."

This took Melba by surprise. People usually discouraged her opinions on anything and everything.

"I'm all ears," she said.

"Well, the problem is this," the mayor said. "I got this real important person comin' to town. You wanna know who it is? It's a secret, but I'll tell you if you promise to help me. But it's gotta stay a secret—you hear?"

"You betcha," said Melba, who was usually as discreet as a blaring army bugle.

"All right—but you gotta keep your trap shut till I make some sort of announcement." He took a deep breath. "You ever heard of . . . Luther Grimes?" he asked dramatically.

There was a long silence.

"No," said Melba at last, somewhat resentfully. Like

Franny's classmates, she too had hoped that the Important Person would be a movie star. "I sure ain't never heard of no Luther Grimes."

"Good Lord, Melba," the mayor said. "What's in those magazines that you're readin' all the time? You're readin' about celebrities and famous people all day long and you don't even know who *Luther Grimes* is?"

"No," Melba repeated sullenly.

The mayor gave out a frustrated sigh. "For your information, Luther Grimes is in the government of the United States. He is none other than one of four hundred and thirty-five members of the House of Repry-sentatives. He repry-sents our very own district here in Skaug County, Minnesota. Yessir, Mr. Grimes is a fine lawmaker and very important man in Washington, D.C.—our nation's exalted capital."

"Oh," said Melba, still not over her disappointment. "How can he be so important if there's four hundred and thirty-five of 'em?"

"He just *is*," yelled the mayor, beginning to be sorry that he had enlisted Melba's help. "Anyway, it ain't him that's comin', it's his wife, Eunice. She's headin' up some fancy literacy commission and she's comin' to town to meet the schoolkids."

"Why don't you git to the point and tell me what yer dern problem *is*," said Melba, her patience dwindling. She began to snap the curlers out of the mayor's hair.

"Ow!" exclaimed the mayor, wincing under Melba's

indelicate touch. "Well—we gotta figure out how to entertain Mrs. Eunice while she's here. I want to show her that Rusty Nail is somethin' real special. Ow! Yessir, we gotta put on a show or somethin'. Lemme ask you this, Melba—what do you think is really special about this fine town? You've lived here all your life. *Ouch!*"

Melba dropped the last of the used curlers into a big plastic bucket and thought. "Well, it used to be the American Coot Capital," she offered.

"I already thought of that," the mayor said. "But we only got about seven of 'em left, and they're all lame. And anyway, how could we put on a show usin' only coots?"

They fell into silence again.

"I know," said Melba. "If she's comin' to see the schoolkids, why don'tcha have them put on a play or somethin'."

"God help us," said the mayor. "Can you imagine Runty Knutson up there on that stage? Why, Eunice Grimes would run out of town faster than a deer with the hunters on its tail. But you might be on to somethin' there. Hmm." He furrowed his brow in deep concentration. Suddenly he leaped up and shouted: "I got it, hallelujah!"

Melba let out a scream, startled by this sudden outburst. "What've you got?" she gasped.

The mayor's eyes bulged with excitement. "I know what the show's gonna be," he said. "First, we'll make the little kids do a play demonstratin' the history of Rusty Nail—a real short, cute version. After that—and this is the good part—we'll just truck that show-off Nancy Orilee up onto the school stage and make her play the pian-er. After all, her parents're always boastin' 'bout how she ain't hit a wrong note in two years.

"And while we're at it," he continued zestily, "we'll make Wes Hansen's kid, Franny, play that old school pian-er too. Maybe we'll make it a contest. Ooh, that's good! We'll bill the town as the home of the musical wonder children! Move over, coots—Rusty Nail is now the Midwestern Capital of Musical Prodigies! That'll blow the boots off ole Eunice! By God, Melba, you're a genius." He threw himself back down into the pink chair, satisfied with his flash of brilliance.

Melba blushed from the compliment as she fluffed up the mayor's hair, which stuck up in parched, indignant tufts all over his head.

"If you think I'm a genius now," she said, "jest you wait until you get in frontuva mirror and see my handiwork, Mayor Reverend. I bet Mizz Eunice will be wantin' a perm of her own."

A secret was nearly impossible to keep in a town as small as Rusty Nail, especially when someone like Melba was the one keeping it.

That evening, after she closed up the Beauty Station, Melba marched eagerly down Main Street. Like a tick ready to burst, she blurted out the secret to the first person she saw: Stella Brunsvold, the popcorn lady. Stella then closed down her popcorn stand and stumped into Elmer's Bar, where she ordered a Pabst Blue Ribbon beer and informed at least six other people about the imminent arrival of Mrs. Eunice Grimes of the literacy commission.

After that, the word spread like wildfire. Soon phones in nearly every living room in Rusty Nail rang. The news reached Franny's house at suppertime as the Hansen family was gnawing through a particularly plasticky meal of dry ham, lumpy mashed potatoes, and overcooked peas. When the phone rang, Franny's dad gratefully shot up from the table to answer it.

After a few minutes, he came back to the table and sat down. "I have some news," he said, pushing his full plate aside. "About Franny."

Oh no, Franny thought. Jessie and Owen looked at each other and groaned.

"Now what'd she do?" Owen said, reaching for his father's unfinished portion. "Hell, Franny, you make me and Jessie look like goody-goodies."

Franny's mother pinched Owen on the arm. "Owen! Do *not* use language like that, especially at the table! What's the news, Wes?" She looked warily at Franny, who slid down her chair under the table.

"That was Elmer down at the bar," Wes said. "Apparently, an important visitor's coming to town. The mayor's going to ask Franny and Nancy Orilee to perform at a school concert in the VIP's honor."

"What?" yelled Jessie. He and Owen hooted. "That's right, Mr. Official—meet our model student, Franny Hansen," Jessie said in a professional-sounding voice. "She's never caused a lick of trouble. The finest and best-behaved girl in all of Minnesota, in fact."

"Our little star—Frances the Talking Mule," Owen added. Francis the Talking Mule was a mule in the movies who did things like join the army and visit haunted houses.

"Don't tease your sister!" exclaimed Lorraine as Franny kicked her brothers' shins under the table. And then, to Franny, she said: "Oh! That's wonderful news, sweetheart! Your first performance." Tears welled in her eyes.

Franny couldn't even say a word. A concert! On stage! How on *earth* had her wish come true? Things like that never happened in Rusty Nail! Maybe her fortunes were changing after all—and this important visitor was clearly her lucky charm.

But then a black thought crossed Franny's mind.

"*Wait* a minute—did you say that both me *and* Nancy are going to be giving the concert?" she asked.

"That's what Elmer said," replied Wes. "But I'm sure we'll find out more tomorrow."

Franny flounced back in her chair. Why did Nancy Orilee have to plague *every* single one of her moments of glory? But after thinking about it for a few minutes, Franny realized that there was a silver lining even to that dark cloud: if Franny played extra well at the concert, she could prove to everyone in Rusty Nail that *she* was a better pianist than Nancy, and put her enemy to shame once and for all.

Wes sat back and beamed. "No dish washing for you tonight, Mozart," he said. "We're real proud of you. Now you'd better hustle over to that piano and practice. It's not going to play itself, you know." He reached over and ruffled her hair.

Franny liked it when her dad called her "Mozart," after the famous composer. Mozart had been so good at the piano that he'd given concerts for kings and queens when he was still a young boy. And now, for the first time, the nickname seemed appropriate.

She ran to the piano and practiced until bedtime.

The next morning, when Franny walked into her classroom, Miss Hamm mildly called her to the front of the room.

"Mr. Moody would like to see you in his office," she said. "It's good news this time."

Franny galloped down the hallway and around the corner to the principal's office. She was dismayed to find Nancy Orilee already standing outside the yellow glass door.

"I don't know why they're asking *you* to play at this concert too," whispered Nancy to Franny. "I guess out of charity or something."

Franny scowled. "You're the prissiest, most spoiled—" she started.

Just at that moment, Mr. Moody whipped his door open.

"What were you saying, Frances Hansen?" he asked, towering over her. Plumes of cigarette smoke wafted out behind him, as though he'd just stepped out of a volcano.

"Nothing," Franny said innocently.

"That's what I thought," he said. "Follow me and close the door." He disappeared back into the haze, sat down at his desk, and informed them that the rumors were true: Mayor Reverend Jerry had asked them to perform at an assembly in honor of an illustrious woman named Mrs. Eunice Grimes.

"Nancy, you'll go first," he said. Nancy smiled smugly and looked over at Franny.

"And you'll wrap things up," he added, pointing a pencil at Franny. "The mayor said this concert is important, so you'd better not botch it up. And no antics up there on the stage, Frances, or you'll be sorry you ever touched a piano."

"*I'll* do a good job, sir," cooed Nancy. "Don't you worry."

Mr. Moody lit another cigarette and coughed. "Both of you better practice hard," he said. "Now beat it. Oh, and break a leg."

When Franny and Nancy got back to their classroom, Miss Hamm had turned out all of the lights, had propped up the old film projector in the back of the room, and was showing the class boring safety cartoons. They had already learned about the perils of playing with matches, and were now being schooled in how to protect themselves in case of a Russian nuclear attack.

Franny slid into her chair and ignored the film, which she'd seen every year since kindergarten. It featured a monkey in a tree holding a stick of dynamite over a turtle, who darted under his shell in the nick of time. A chorus sang along cheerfully:

> *There was a turtle by the name of*
> *Bert,*
> *And Bert the turtle was very alert.*
> *When danger threatened him,*
> *he never got hurt.*
> *He knew just what to do. . . .*
> *He ducked!*
> *And covered!*

After the cartoon, a man showed a bunch of kids in a classroom like Franny's how to hide under their desks if their town was ever bombed.

"You'll hear an explosion like you've never heard before," he threatened.

Just then, Runty Knutson let out a terrific belch. All of the kids shrieked with laughter, and several of the other boys began a burping contest. Miss Hamm was beside herself as she tried to restore order.

Franny took advantage of the distraction to tell Sandy about her conference with Mr. Moody.

Sandy let out a whoop of excitement. "Hot diggity-dog!" she exclaimed. "In front of the whole school and town? Wow, wow, wow!"

At lunchtime, the girls took their trays out into the schoolyard, where they could discuss the development privately.

"You know, Franny—this could be your big chance," Sandy said as she peeled a piece of salmon-colored bologna out of her sandwich and threw it on the ground. "And it's better that you're goin' last in the concert, because you'll be the one everyone remembers. I bet Mr. Moody planned it that way because he knows you're better than Prancy. You'd better practice real hard this week."

"I know," said Franny. "I'm going to. I want Nancy to look like she's playing a washboard next to me."

"Well, *that* won't be hard," Sandy said. "She plays like an old player piano. The notes are always right, but it's still real borin' to listen to. Not like you. You play like a pro."

Franny nearly blushed at the rare compliment, but then Sandy gave her a grave look.

"But you'd better remember that this isn't just about

Prancy," she continued. "What if this famous Eunice woman thinks that you're the best piano player she ever heard? She might even bring you back to Washington, D.C., to play for the president—like that girl we saw in that newsreel, remember? You could get rich and famous for real. Just don't blow it, 'cause this might be your only shot—like when your dad met that jazz guy, Duke."

Of course, these had been Franny's thoughts exactly. Eunice Grimes was being sent to Rusty Nail to turn Franny into the Mozart of her generation. Her fingers automatically began to drum out her mainstay Bach piece on her knees. Her thoughts speeded up, and she wished that she could go home early to practice. Maybe she could even convince Wes and Lorraine to let her stay home from school for a few days to get some extra rehearsal time in.

After all, her very future was at stake.

Chapter Four

The people of Rusty Nail prepared for the arrival of Mrs. Eunice Grimes as though she was the Queen of England. They mowed grass and hosed down the barn animals. All of the bicycles and Big Wheels that usually littered the town's front lawns were stacked up behind closed garage doors. Rickety old Hans Zimmerman, who owned the grocery shop on Main Street, got so excited that he decorated the entire storefront with big Christmas lights and plastic snowmen and Santas.

The women of the Rusty Nail Charter of the Homemakers Association of America prepared a bountiful mountain of baked goods for the occasion: cupcakes, carrot cakes, banana cakes, molasses cakes, cookies of every imaginable variety, an intimidating armada of pies, and an assortment of quivering Jell-O molds with pieces of canned fruit suspended in their gelatinous bellies.

Shoes were shined, and shirts and dresses ironed. Down at the Smitty Beauty Station, Miss Norma Smitty and Melba could hardly keep up with the townspeople's beautifying needs. From dawn to dusk, they shaved faces, rolled up curlers, and lacquered fingernails.

Mayor Reverend Jerry gave a special sermon in church that Sunday, declaring that God had sent Mrs. Eunice Grimes to the town so that she, and subsequently the rest of the world, would learn what a model community Rusty Nail was.

"If you wanna see real America, you won't find it in Hollywood," he thundered to his congregation. "And you won't find it starin' up at the fancy skyscrapers in New York City neither—no sir. Real America is right here in Rusty Nail, with its corn and big sky and honest, regular folks who work with their hands. Towns like ours are the heart of the nation and the bulwarks against the Commie Menace! And now's our chance to show off fer the rest of the country, hallelujah!"

After school every day that week, Franny had gone to Mrs. Staudt's house to get ready. Her teacher had picked out a Mozart piece at Franny's insistence, and for the first time in her life, Franny practiced during every moment of her free time. She started to feel that she *understood* the music somehow. The notes became words and the phrases turned into sentences and the sentences into stories. She imagined the expression on Mozart's face as he wrote the piece and played it, and she crooked her fingers as she imagined that he would. When she wasn't actually practicing, she was *thinking* about practicing. She even dreamt about music each night.

Each afternoon, Mrs. Staudt watched Franny play the piano with admiration, her bloodshot eyes glistening and her cigarette burning. Even her decrepit father seemed to respect the gravity of the situation, because he didn't make a single cameo appearance.

Finally, the day before the concert, her teacher said to Franny: "Well, you've sure made progress, girlie, and you're all ready for the big day. And furthermore, you've learned everything I can teach you. After this concert, your parents are going to have to find you a better teacher."

"What?" said Franny. "Who's going to teach me, then? My parents can't afford that guy who teaches Nancy Orilee."

Mrs. Staudt shrugged. "I dunno," she said. "I'm sure something will come up." And she ushered Franny to the front door.

Franny marched home, clutching her music books. *Somewhere in Minnesota,* she thought, *Mrs. Eunice what's-her-name is getting ready to come down to Rusty Nail, and she has no idea what she's going to find here: me!*

But questions plagued her too: Would she have to leave right away for Washington, and if so, could she bring her parents or Sandy along? When would she come back?

For that matter, *would* she come back at all, or would she be expected to just keep going around the world, giving concerts and impressing other presidents, kings, and queens?

When she turned onto Main Street and glanced up at her apartment, her heart nearly froze, for clouds of black smoke billowed out of the kitchen window on the second floor. In a panic, she rushed to the building and shouted up to her mother again and again. Soon the living-room window opened and Lorraine stuck her head out.

"It's okay, sweetheart," she called down to her daughter. "I just had a little accident in the kitchen. Come on upstairs—it's clearing out in here now."

Franny let out a breath of relief and ran up the stairs. Lorraine stood in the kitchen, waving a baking sheet over a completely charred pie.

"Mom! What were you *doing*?" Franny wailed. "You know you can't cook pies."

"Well," said Lorraine, embarrassed. "All of the other mothers are bringing desserts to the concert, so I thought that I'd make something too. It's blueberry." She peered down at the black pastry. "Do you think I could still serve it? I bet I could scrape the burned part off the top."

"*Please* don't bring it," Franny begged. "I have enough things to worry about." She stalked down the hazy hallway and into her bedroom, which also smelled of smoke and burned crust. Franny scowled and wrenched her window up to air it out.

"Sorry about that, honey," Lorraine said, appearing in the doorway. "I guess the oven must be broken or something. Say, what were you planning on wearing to the concert?"

"Mom, there's nothing wrong with the oven; you *always* burn pies," Franny snapped. "And I guess I'll just wear my jeans and my favorite yellow shirt."

Franny's mother hesitated. Then she said: "Tomorrow is going to be a very important day, Franny. And I think that you should wear something special to mark the occasion."

"Like what?" Franny asked suspiciously.

Lorraine smiled. "Just a minute," she said excitedly, and disappeared into the hallway.

A few moments later, she returned with a shopping bag, which she handed to Franny. "Surprise! I bought you a new dress."

Oh Lord, Franny thought with despair as she pulled the dress out of the bag. Checkered with white and blue squares, it had big ruffles attached to the shoulders and the hem. It reminded Franny of Dorothy's getup in the movie *The Wizard of Oz.*

"Do you like it, honey?" Lorraine asked.

Franny almost burst into tears. "Can't I just wear the jeans?" She hastily tried to think of a reason why she couldn't wear the dress. "It's just, um, easier for me to work the piano pedals when I wear pants," she said.

"Oh, don't be silly," said Franny's mother carelessly as

she fluffed up the ruffles. "This is perfect. You're going to look so special!"

Franny grew desperate. "Mom! Please don't make me wear it! Everyone will laugh at me," she blurted out.

Lorraine frowned and put her hands on her hips. "Frances Hansen!" she said. "I drove all forty miles to La Crosse this morning to pick that dress up for you. Everyone in Rusty Nail will be at the concert, and I don't want you to look like a raggedy tomboy. You're going to wear the dress tomorrow, and that's all there is to it!"

Once her mother's hands went to her hips, Franny knew that the battle was over. When Lorraine was determined about something, she could not be budged. Underneath her sweetness was a core of steel.

Franny threw herself down on her bed and rolled over on her side with her back to her mother.

"Fine," she said fiercely to the wall. "Tomorrow when I get up onto the stage and everyone laughs at me, it'll be *your* fault. And I'll never be able to go back to school again as long as I live, and that will be your fault too. And that Eunice woman is going to leave me behind when she goes to Washington—all because of the dress."

Lorraine looked confused. "Why would Mrs. Grimes take you along to Washington?" she asked.

"Never mind," said Franny quickly, muffling her face in the pillow. "All I know is that if you make me wear that dress, my life is going to be over."

Lorraine suppressed a laugh. "Maybe you should have

been an actress instead of a pianist," she said. "Now, I'm going to rescue that pie and make supper before your father comes home." She trotted out of the bedroom and closed the door.

Franny rolled over and glared hatefully at the frilly dress hanging on the back of her desk chair.

Tomorrow is either going to be the best day of my life, she thought, *or the worst.*

Chapter Five

The big day arrived at last. Sandy waited for Franny outside the school before the bell rang.

"Oh, *brother*," Sandy said when she saw the checkered dress—which, incidentally, still reeked of smoke. "Maybe we should spill something on it so you'd get to go home and change," she offered helpfully.

Franny considered this for a moment. "I can't," she concluded. "My mother would kill me."

She trudged into the school, her shoulder ruffles fluttering in the breeze, and plunked herself down at her desk. The assembly for Mrs. Eunice Grimes was scheduled for twelve noon. Franny would have to tolerate four whole hours of humiliation and anxiety before the concert.

Runty Knutson stuck his nose in the air and sniffed

noisily. "Why does it smell like smoke in here? Hey, maybe the school is burning down!" he shouted hopefully.

All of the other kids sniffed the air and looked around. Franny slunk down lower in her seat. Then Nancy Orilee sailed in. To Franny's dismay, her rival looked fantastic in a new red dress, shining black Mary Jane shoes, and a velvet beret. She must have slept in curlers the night before, because her hair hung in perfect ringlets around her face.

"Good morning, Sandy Anne," Nancy said in her nasal voice as she sat down at her desk. She grinned when she looked in Franny's direction. "And good morning, Dorothy. Where's Toto? *Oh!* It's you, Frances. I didn't recognize you. Is that a leftover Halloween costume or something?"

Franny gritted her teeth and drummed her fingers on her knees. *I'm not going to let that spoiled brat steal the day,* she said to herself over and over. She watched the minute hand click slowly around the face of the clock, and the morning stretched out like long, sticky taffy in front of her. She went over the Mozart piece again and again in her head, the notes mixing with the rhythmic sound of the clock until she practically fell into a trance.

Suddenly someone poked her in the ribs.

"Franny!" Sandy said excitedly, standing over her. "Get up—it's time to go." Franny leaped out of her chair, practically knocking it over.

"Line up in two lines, children," Miss Hamm squeaked. "Boys on one side and girls on the other."

"What about *that*?" yelled Runty, pointing at Gretchen

Beasley. "Which line should Gretchen be in, since no one knows if it's a boy or a girl?" Predictably, Gretchen burst into tears.

"Ohhh," wailed Miss Hamm, looking desperate. "*Please* be good, Runty." She shepherded Gretchen to the girls' line. Then Sandy shoved Runty into the girls' line, and mayhem broke out. Miss Hamm finally gave up and herded the class out into the hallway mob-style.

A great crowd milled around outside the doors to the auditorium. To the right of the entrance stood six folding tables, heaving under the weight of the cakes and pies brought by all of the mothers. Franny's palms sweated when the people walked into the auditorium, which seemed as hot as a boiler room inside. The ceiling fans spun crazily, and everyone fanned themselves with sheets of paper.

Nearly every Polk School student and Rusty Nail resident was there, waiting to make an all-American impression on Mrs. Eunice Grimes. A big, hand-painted banner hung above the stage, declaring:

MRS. EUNICE GRIMES

WELCOME TO RUSTY NAIL

WE COOTN'T BE HAPPIER TO SEE YOU

Below it, Mr. Moody paced nervously back and forth. When he saw Franny and Nancy come in, he waved for them to come to the front of the auditorium. Franny felt like royalty as she sat down in the first row. Suddenly Mr. Moody sniffed the air.

"What smells like smoke?" he said. He glared down at Franny and leaned in toward her. "It's you!" His eyes narrowed. "You horrid child. You better not have been smoking a cigarette on school premises on the biggest day in recent Rusty Nail history!"

"I didn't!" Franny squawked defensively. "It's my dress—I swear! My mother set a pie on fire in our house last night and the dress still smells like smoke."

Mr. Moody reluctantly accepted this explanation. Even he knew of Lorraine's famous culinary disasters.

Nancy snickered. When Mr. Moody was looking in the other direction, she leaned in toward Franny and sang under her breath:

> It's Francis the Talking Mule,
> Hee haw, hee haw,
> Eating dirty straw.
> A mule is a fool.

Without thinking, Franny furiously tore out a sheet of her music book, quickly crumpled it into a ball, and threw it right in Nancy's face. Nancy was just about to raise a fuss when a voice from the back of the auditorium crowed:

"Here she comes!"

The sound of creaking seats filled the room as everyone turned around or stood up or craned their necks to get a look. Suddenly the crowd near the doors parted and Mayor Reverend Jerry swept in majestically.

"Fine folks," he said, his face and frizzy new curls glistening with perspiration. "It's been a real long time since we've had such an important guest in this town. Let's give a big Rusty Nail welcome to Mrs. Eunice Grimes of the Minnesota Commission on Literacy!"

Everyone clapped and hooted. Then the crowd parted just a little further and into the room squeezed the fattest woman Franny had ever seen. She wore a terribly crabby expression above her numerous chins. Not even looking at the audience, she trucked down the aisle to the front of the room. Mayor Reverend Jerry scrambled after her, and after him came Mrs. Grimes' assistant, a man as thin and brittle as a piece of spaghetti.

Finally, the party reached the front of the room. "Where'm I supposed to sit?" Mrs. Grimes grunted to Mr. Moody, without so much as a hello.

"Right here, ma'am." Mayor Reverend Jerry stepped in, waving graciously to one of the empty front-row seats. "But we were hopin' you'd say a few words to the townspeople first."

Mrs. Eunice Grimes peered down at the narrow old seat. "Is this some sorta cruel joke? That's not gonna do it, boys," she snapped. "Guess I'm just gonna have to stand up."

Mr. Moody and Mayor Reverend Jerry made the hasty decision to run next door to the third-grade classroom and haul in a desk, upon which Mrs. Grimes could sit. The visitor glared at it and her hosts as she clumped up to the front of the stage. Everyone leaned forward with great anticipation to hear what she was going to say.

"Glad to be here," she said grudgingly, and nodded once.

That was all! She plodded over to the desk and sat down on it. Her scrap of an assistant tapped his wristwatch and squeaked to Mr. Moody: "We have to be in Harmonyville in an hour. Do you think we could speed things up?"

"Right!" said Mr. Moody, clapping his hands. "Let's begin with the entertainment, shall we?"

The fourth grade rushed out onto the stage and performed a theatrical history of Rusty Nail. This riveting play included only the most important developments of the town's history: the finding of the old, bent pioneer nails, the first corn harvest, the first annual American coot festival, and the building of the town bar, Elmer's.

Franny snuck a look at Mrs. Grimes toward the end of the play. Was this *really* the person who would make her into a famous pianist? This whole event certainly seemed different in spirit from her father's experience with Duke Ellington years before. Mrs. Grimes' eyes had glazed over, and she looked like she wished that she was anyplace besides a school in Rusty Nail.

At long last, the finale of the play came with a great crashing of cymbals. The audience stood up and cheered as the actors took many bows. Mrs. Eunice Grimes heaved herself off the teetering desk.

"Well, that's that," she said, gesturing to her assistant to leave. "Let's go, Wilmer. Thanks, boys," she said to Mayor Reverend Jerry and Mr. Moody, who looked panicked.

"Oh no," cried the mayor quickly, cutting in front of her. "We still got quite a treat in store for you. You might've thought that Rusty Nail was famous only for its coots and fine grains and corn. But we also manufacture something else that's pretty darn special: child musical geniuses. This here is Nancy Orilee and Franny Hansen. They're both gonna play the pian-er for you."

Mrs. Grimes' assistant tapped his watch again. "We only have ten minutes," he sniveled. Mrs. Grimes sighed again and sat back down on the desk.

Mr. Moody hustled Nancy up onto the stage. "Hurry up," he whispered loudly to her.

Nancy set up her sheet music on the school's old, defeated-looking upright piano and gingerly sat down on the bench. She smiled at the audience.

"I will be playing a piece by a composer named Schumann, who is one of my favorites," she announced.

True to her reputation, Nancy didn't hit a single wrong note. Franny listened impatiently to her rival, whose playing somehow reminded her of fussy paper doilies and tea parties. Not a tea party like the wild, wonderful one in *Alice in Wonderland*, but rather a mean great-aunt's tea party that no one in her right mind would want to attend. *There's no feeling in Prancy's playing*, Franny thought, her throat tightening with anticipation. *No feeling at all, no oomph. I can do so much better than that.*

Dink, dink, dink went the piano as Nancy methodically played her piece. When she finally finished, she stood up and curtsied daintily as a ballerina. Franny rolled her eyes, but everyone else in the room applauded quite enthusiastically. Even Mrs. Grimes clapped her paws together a few times.

"Franny!" hissed Mr. Moody. "It's your turn—on the double!"

Franny scrambled up out of her seat and ran onto the stage. As she sat down at the piano, she glanced at Mrs. Grimes. The woman wasn't even paying any attention to her, concentrating instead on some sort of buzzing fly. Franny's heart sank. She simply *had* to outdo Nancy Orilee and capture the imagination of Mrs. Eunice Grimes, and that's all there was to it.

She opened her music book with a great flourish—and got a nasty shock. The first page of her piece was missing.

In horror, she looked down at the floor and saw the paper she'd crumpled up and thrown in Nancy's face—and of *course* it was her music sheet. That was just her luck, as usual. Panic set in.

"Any day now, Frances," said Mr. Moody, his eyebrows

raised menacingly. Someone in the audience began tapping his foot. Even the ceiling fans whirred impatiently.

Franny took a deep breath to calm herself down. She had no choice but to play the piece from memory. *Like a real pianist,* she told herself. *All of the famous ones know their music by heart.* She felt stronger then, and stood up to face the audience.

"I'm playing a short piece by Mozart," she squeaked. A burst of applause erupted in Miss Hamm's section, and Franny saw her teacher hushing Sandy and Runty.

Franny sat back down abruptly and closed her eyes for a moment. Suddenly she could see the missing page in her mind. She put her hands on the keys and began to play.

The school piano was quite out of tune, but Franny imagined that she was playing on a fine, huge grand piano, and slowly the bent, tinny notes corrected themselves in her imagination. How wonderfully natural it felt to be up on the stage! She leaned into the keyboard, as she imagined a passionate, world-famous pianist would. Instead of making her nervous, the gaze of hundreds excited her. She had never felt so *right* before—like a fish that finds its way into the ocean after spending its whole life in a little stream. She played more beautifully than ever. When she finished the finale at last, she stood up triumphantly and took a deep, dramatic bow.

To her horror, no one clapped. Every person in Rusty Nail stared up at her in silence. For a second, Franny wondered if she was having a nightmare.

And then, at this darkest of all dark moments, the audience burst into wild applause. Several people even stood up. And then everyone else followed suit, still clapping hard.

Franny had gotten the first standing ovation of her career! Then she caught a glimpse of her father and mother in the back of the room. Her mother dabbed at her eyes with a white hanky, and her father was standing and clapping with all of his might. Not knowing what else to do, Franny bowed again and again.

All of a sudden, Nancy Orilee stood up and stomped back up onto the stage. The room buzzed with confusion and surprise.

"What are you *doing*, young lady?" exclaimed Mr. Moody. "Get back here, or you'll have detention until you graduate from high school." Mrs. Grimes' assistant was tapping his watch so hard that Franny thought he would break the glass face.

"I'm going to play an encore," Nancy announced, and before anyone could protest, she sat down at the piano and began to play. Everyone in the audience looked at each other in astonishment as she pounded away at the keys. The result was another flawlessly played Schumann piece. All the while, Franny stood there on the stage awkwardly, not knowing what to do or where to go. Nancy excitedly finished at last, shot up off the bench, and curtsied.

This time, everyone stood up and clapped for her as

well, except for a few loud boos from the back of the room. Miss Hamm had clearly not managed to subdue Runty and Sandy.

Franny's face felt as though it was on fire. *Not this time, Prancy,* she thought wildly. *I'm going to win and you're not going to stop me.*

"I have an encore too!" she shouted over the applause, and she marched over to the piano. "Move it," she said to Nancy, and sat down on the bench, hands on the keyboard.

Suddenly, she drew a blank. What *was* her encore? She had only practiced this one Mozart piece for the concert. Then she saw Mrs. Staudt in the back of the room and had a brilliant idea. Why, she would play that old Bach piece that they'd studied week after week! She'd played it so many times that it would be as easy as breathing. *Ho, ho,* she thought. *Now you're going to get it, Nancy Orilee.*

Franny began to play with the zeal of a soldier in battle. The old Bach piece had never sounded so defiant before. Mrs. Staudt grew very excited in the back row. When Franny finished, she stood up again, and everyone applauded yet again.

Mr. Moody rushed up onto the stage and slammed down the lid over the keyboard.

"My goodness!" he said, glaring viciously at Franny and Nancy. He looked like he badly needed a cigarette. "Who ever would have known that Rusty Nail had such talented pianists?"

Everyone clapped and whooped again. Mayor Reverend Jerry joined Mr. Moody on the stage.

"Well, Your Excellency," he said to Mrs. Grimes. "Bet you've never heard such fine playin'. I'm sure you now know what a special community this is. Would you like to say a few more words to the folks of Rusty Nail?"

Franny's mind raced as she waited for the visitor's response. She knew that she'd played perfectly. She was almost sure that Mrs. Grimes would ask her to come back to Washington, D.C., with her on this very day. She felt a rush of shame at the idea of leaving her parents behind, but she was sure they'd understand, especially Wes. Looking at Nancy across the stage, Franny bet that her rival was having similar thoughts.

Mrs. Grimes lurched off the desk for the last time that day and wheezed as she climbed the stairs to the stage. Franny held her breath as Mrs. Grimes came and stood next to her.

"This girl's a good piano player," the woman said to the audience, clapping Franny on the shoulder rather roughly. "And the other one's not so bad either. But Rusty Nail's real talent is the bake sale outside. D'ya mind if we take some cakes to go?" She signaled to her assistant, who scurried out the auditorium doors toward the food-laden tables in the hallway. "Not that god-awful burned pie," Mrs. Grimes shouted after him.

The room went silent again as the townspeople gaped at her.

"Well, thanks a lot, mister," Mrs. Eunice Grimes said, and clapped Mr. Moody on the back too. "Your school appears to be literate to me. I'll make sure to put that in my report. It's been swell."

And with that, she nodded at Mayor Reverend Jerry and stomped down the stairs and up the aisle to the exit.

"But you ain't heard even *one* of the kids read!" sputtered the surprised mayor. But Mrs. Eunice Grimes had already left the room. Mayor Reverend Jerry faced the audience. "Um, well, all righty, then. I guess this concert's over, folks. Let's all go get somethin' to eat. Amen." He scuttled off the stage after the guest of honor.

Franny stood dumbfounded on the stage in front of the piano and watched Mrs. Grimes leave the room. Her Duke Ellington moment had come and gone forever, just like her father's before her. Why had she ever allowed her expectations to get so high in the first place? She should have known better. Nothing amazing or miraculous ever happened to the people who lived in Rusty Nail.

She looked up at the ceiling, refusing to cry in front of the whole town like that baby Gretchen Beasley. With as much dignity as she could muster, she collected her music book from the piano and stiffly walked down the stairs of the stage. Her parents rushed up to her.

"I swear, Franny," said her father excitedly. "That was the best thing I've ever heard! You should have seen their faces." He gripped her in a hard, proud hug.

A tear slid down Franny's nose, and Wes saw it before

she could wipe it away. "What's the matter, Mozart? You were great!" he exclaimed.

Franny lowered her chin into her chest. "She didn't like it," she whispered to her dad.

"*Who* didn't?" asked Wes.

"Mrs. Grimes," Franny answered. "She didn't ask me to come away with her to play in Washington or all over the country, like Duke Ellington asked you."

Wes and Lorraine looked at each other in surprise. After a moment, Wes took a deep breath.

"That was different, baby," he said, putting his hand on Franny's head. "Mrs. Grimes isn't in a jazz band— she's just a silly woman whose husband is a politician. She probably doesn't know the difference between a hen and a rooster, much less the difference between a decent pianist and a wonderful one."

None of these condolences cheered Franny, whose chin wobbled and cheeks stung under her salty tears. She felt as though someone had given her a beautifully wrapped present that had secretly been filled with grimy rocks and worms. Her plans and aspirations didn't simply wilt; they crashed down on top of her like an avalanche.

Wes put his arms around his daughter's shoulders.

"Chin up, Mozart," he said. "You were wonderful— really." He leaned in and said quietly into Franny's ear: "And everyone was whispering about how much better you were than Nancy. We all know where the real talent is. Now let's go get us some cake and greet your fans."

Lorraine wiped Franny's cheeks with her hanky, and they walked out of the crowded auditorium and into the hallway. Mrs. Eunice Grimes was already gone, having taken several pies, a Jell-O mold, and a banana bread to eat on the road. Everyone congratulated Franny on her fine performance.

As she walked through the stifling horde of people, clutching a paper cup of Hawaiian Punch, Franny didn't really hear or see anything around her. She had become suddenly, acutely, unhappily aware that to the eyes of an outsider, she completely blended in with the rest of the townspeople of Rusty Nail. Just as a single instrument blends into a huge orchestra.

And at that moment, it seemed that she was destined to stay that way forever.

Part II

Adagio

Chapter Six

About a week after the Eunice Grimes affair, Franny and Sandy trudged out to Mr. Klompenhower's farm to repair his broken pig barn. This was how they were going to pay him back for ruining his chicken cart during the water-balloon debacle.

When they got there, they discovered that the barn needed to have a whole new wall nailed up to its bare frame.

"Ha—this is no big deal," Sandy announced as she squinted up at the wall. "A baby could do it. But I'm gonna take my time in puttin' this ole barn back together."

"Why?" said Franny, swatting at a pesty swarm of flies. "I just want to get it over with."

"So you can go home and mope even more about Eunice Grimes?" Sandy said. "Forget about her, willya? She was just a fat old donkey who didn't know her elbow from her knee. It was a false alarm—she was a fake Duke Ellington. Maybe someday soon a *real* Duke Ellington–type person is gonna come to Rusty Nail and see how good you are—and then things'll get rollin'.'"

"Fat chance," said Franny glumly. "People in this dumb town don't get second chances, you know. In case you forgot: you said so yourself."

"Go ahead—pout if you wanna," Sandy said, fishing around in her backpack for something. "But wait till you see what I've got here."

She pulled out a sheath of comic books and a big plastic bag filled with candy: four Big Choice bubble gum cigars, candy cigarettes and necklaces, Chick-O-Sticks, Fun Dip packets, cinnamon Hot Tamales, a box of Junior Mints, some Mallo Cups, sixteen Pixy Stix, two sets of Wax Lips, a handful of Atomic Fireballs, three Charleston Chews, some Dubble Bubble, some Root Beer Barrels, a Saf-T-Pop, a Slo Poke, and, of course, Red Hots.

"Where did you get all of that?" Franny asked. "I thought your parents took all of your candy away when you got grounded."

"They did," said Sandy smugly. "But they never found the ole Halloween stash that I kept in the back of my closet. It always pays to have an emergency supply." She popped an Atomic Fireball into her mouth and promptly spat it out. "*Dang,* that's hot. See, the longer it takes us to fix the barn, the longer I have to eat this stash in private. Want a Charleston Chew?"

Franny admired Sandy's craftiness, but the thought of eating year-old candy made her stomach clench up. Plus, the smell of the pigpen inside was absolutely revolting; it practically colored the air yellow and brown.

"No thanks—you should have it," she said.

"Suit yourself." Sandy shrugged.

"I'll just slap a few boards up onto the wall so it looks like we've been doing something out here," Franny said. Mr. Klompenhower had left a stack of new boards, a tin of nails, and two old hammers next to the wall. Franny hauled up a plank and some nails. A dirty pig waddled out of the barn and stared dimly at her.

"You know," said Sandy, tossing the Atomic Fireball to the pig, who immediately gobbled it up, "this could actually be a lucky break for you. Think about it. You always hated your piano lessons, and then Mrs. Staudt tells you she can't teach you anymore. Then Mrs. Grimes turns out to be a phony Duke Ellington and leaves town without takin' you along. Maybe it's a sign."

Franny stopped pounding a nail and looked at Sandy. "What kind of sign?" she asked.

"Maybe that you're meant to be just a regular girl—

like me, I guess," said Sandy. "I mean, you're real good at the piano and all, but maybe it's not meant to be or somethin'. And after all, now that you don't have lessons anymore, you have tons of free time after school just to fool around."

Franny sat down in the dirt. The pig grunted, snot dripping from its snout onto the ground.

"Part of me wants to just mess around with you and Runty all the time," she said. "And sure, I hated my lessons. But that's just because Mrs. Staudt was such a bad teacher. I like playing. I'd feel real strange if I just stopped."

"Why?" asked Sandy in exasperation. "It's just a big pain in the neck for you."

Franny bristled. How could she explain to Sandy what playing the piano really felt like? "I don't know. I just *get* it—the music, I mean," she said. "And I liked being up on stage, and I even liked practicing before the concert, because this time there was a point to it. There never was a point before, and after what happened at the concert, I feel like there's no point now either."

"Well, you can always play at the church," Sandy offered. "You know, on Sundays and at weddings and funerals and stuff like that."

Franny scowled. It seemed terribly unfair that she was facing such a dead end. If a boy wanted to be a farmer in Rusty Nail, there were dozens of people to show him how to milk a cow or till a field. If a girl wanted to be a house-wife, flocks of women clamored to be her mentor. But if a girl wanted to be a famous pianist—or *anything* exceptional for that matter—her chances were bleak as winter sleet. She stood up abruptly.

"I don't *want* to play in church," she said spitefully, picking up the hammer. And with that, she gave a nail in the board an extra-hard whack and then another and another. The last whack missed the nail and came down on her thumb instead. She threw down the hammer and shrieked.

Sandy jumped up to examine her friend's injured finger.

"Can you move it?" she asked.

Franny nodded miserably. "Just barely," she whimpered, feeling very sorry for herself.

"I bet it's just going to get all big and purple," Sandy predicted. "We'd better get you some ice. Jeez, Franny, this just isn't your week."

A few days later, on Sunday morning, Lorraine woke Franny, Jessie, and Owen up early to go to church, a weekly pilgrimage that bored Franny senseless. In addition to sitting through an endless sermon by Mayor Reverend Jerry, Franny had to stick around afterward while Lorraine gossiped with the matrons of Rusty Nail in what Franny's dad called "the Colosseum," or the back room of the church. Once, Franny had asked him why he called it that.

"Well, as you should have learned in school by now, the Colosseum is an ancient stadium in Rome where, two thousand years ago, defenseless people were forced to fight snarling, hungry lions," Wes had explained. "And everyone in Rome lined up for miles to get inside and watch. It was like their version of Hauser's Movie Palace. Now, the way I see it, the back room of the church is a remarkably similar venue, except that people there fall victim to bloodthirsty gossip instead of vicious lions.

"And, frankly, I'd rather get eaten by a lion than have one bite of coffee cake in that snake pit," he'd added before Lorraine had shooed him away.

Today, the second she walked with her mother into the Colosseum after the sermon, Franny knew that some new and especially juicy item of gossip crowned the menu. Miss Norma Smitty held court in the middle of the room, surrounded by a gaggle of women. Lorraine helped herself to some coffee and gave Franny a slice of dry brown-sugar crumble.

"Come on, honey," Lorraine said, dragging Franny toward the crowd. She wedged herself next to Mrs. Charity Engebraten on the outer rung of onlookers, a position akin to nosebleed seats in the real Colosseum.

"What's Norma quacking about now, Charity?" asked Lorraine, sipping her lukewarm Sanka.

"Well," said Mrs. Engebraten. "According to Norma, Rusty Nail's gettin' a newcomer."

"My goodness," said Lorraine. "Twice in a week? Another visitor like Eunice Grimes?"

"No, nothing like that," said Mrs. Engebraten. "This one's comin' to stay. They say that Charlie Koenig went off and got himself a wife. Can you believe it?"

"Really!" said Lorraine, her eyebrows raised. "Well, I never."

Charlie Koenig was Rusty Nail's young lawyer, whose clapboard office sat next to Wes's on Main Street. He was the closest thing that Rusty Nail had to royalty, being the only child of the town's former mayor Ludwig Koenig. His mother had died in childbirth with Charlie, and his dad died when Charlie was just finishing high school.

All his life, Charlie had mostly kept to himself, and soon after his father's death, he had shocked the town by getting a fancy scholarship to a hoity-toity university out East. Then he shocked everyone again by staying out there and going to an even swankier law school in New York City, and shocked them all yet *again* by coming back to Rusty Nail to set up shop afterward. No one quite knew why, but Wes told Franny once that Charlie just really loved the big Minnesota sky and open spaces he'd grown up with.

As a grown man, he was as private as he'd been as a kid, and he didn't mingle with the town folks very often.

Such aloofness was practically a sin in a town that churned out a demanding social schedule of church dinners, bingo tournaments, tag sales, and farm-equipment fairs.

But Charlie's good-humored smile and nice ways won over even those who were inclined to call him snobby. People gradually put aside their suspicions of Mr. City Slicker (as Norma Smitty had nicknamed him) and hired him to settle land quarrels and bill disputes. And as he started to make a little money, the single ladies in town suddenly began to wonder why he wasn't married.

Mrs. Engebraten and Lorraine leaned forward into the group just in time to hear Norma Smitty announce with great relish: "And I haven't even told you the big news yet—guess where she's from? I'll give you a hint—it ain't America, that's fer sure."

A deafening cacophony followed: "Whaddya mean?" "A foreigner movin' *here* to Rusty Nail?" "You don't say!"

"What's wrong with the women here in Rusty Nail?" grumbled Melba the salon assistant. "Don't see why Charlie has t' go all the way to another country t' find himself a good wife."

Oh, who cares, *you old billy goats,* thought Franny sulkily, and wondered why Sandy hadn't come in yet with her mother. Her thumb throbbed under its big cartoonish bandage.

"Just try to guess where she's from," Norma said,

dangling the answer in front of the crowd like a big succulent steak.

All of the women concurred that the newcomer had to be from Sweden or Norway. After all, *everyone* in Rusty Nail had ancestors from those countries. The town had been a big, potato-filled Scandinavian outpost for decades.

"Wrong!" crowed Norma, and her eyes narrowed with malice. "She's *Russian*! Jest imagine—a Commie right here in Rusty Nail, in the heartland of America! In the coot capital of the country."

"*Former* coot capital," someone reminded her as the rest of the women gasped all at once.

"And not only *that*," Norma Smitty continued. "*They say* that she and Charlie're already married—and you can bet that the ceremony wasn't in no church either! Those Commies are a godless bunch, you know. Anyway, Charlie went back out East on a business trip and *eloped* with that woman in New York City. Word is that they're off on their honeymoon, and that he's bringin' her back here real soon. Yessir, the Cold War's a-comin' right here t' our doorsteps."

"What does *elope* mean?" Franny whispered to Lorraine.

"Eloping is when a couple runs away and gets married without having a big wedding," Lorraine said distractedly.

"Why are they letting a Commie come here?" Franny pestered her mother. "Aren't they all supposed to be over in Russia, figuring out how to shoot nuclear missiles at us?"

Lorraine peered down at her daughter. "Why don't you run along and see if Sandy is out in the yard?" she asked, and bustled Franny toward the exit. "I'll be out once I finish my coffee." And she turned her attention back to the mob.

Franny walked outside and stood at the top of the stairs, blinking in the harsh noon sunshine.

"A spy!" shouted Norma from the middle of the circus inside. "The new wife's gotta be a spy. I'm willin' to bet m' shop on it. That's the only reason a Commie comes to a town like this. What was Charlie *thinkin'*?"

And with that, all of the women began talking at once again, gabbing like a bunch of agitated hens.

Wow, thought Franny. *A Russian spy in Rusty Nail, of all places!* She ran down the stairs to find Sandy and tell her the news.

Under normal circumstances, the residents of Rusty Nail discussed a fairly limited roster of topics: crop prices, droughts, how much they loved President Eisenhower and hated Democrat Adlai Stevenson, and, last but *certainly* not least: each other. Closed doors and drawn curtains never sealed in secrets, which inevitably seeped out through keyholes and around the edges of the loose windowpanes. Everyone knew *everything* about everyone else—and when information was vague, rumors and speculation cemented the gaps between the bricks.

After Norma Smitty's announcement at the Colosseum, the town's number one topic of discussion was the bizarre betrayal by Charlie Koenig and the impending arrival of his Commie wife.

"I always knew there was somethin' not quite right about ole Charlie," Elmer the bartender said to his customers once the news hit the streets. "A man who doesn't drink beer with the rest of the fellas has gotta have somethin' t' hide."

"Well, he's always been real odd," said Rodney the jail janitor from behind his dented beer can. "But I never woulda guessed that he'd do somethin' like this, bein' born and bred right here in Rusty Nail."

At that moment, Mr. Arflot, the owner of the saddle store, was galloping down to the town hall to inform the mayor of the development. When he heard what was happening, Mayor Reverend Jerry drummed his fingers on his desk and contemplated the problem.

"We could build a big fence around their house, with a watchtower," suggested Mr. Arflot excitedly. Too flat-footed and nearsighted to have joined the army, Mr. Arflot was thrilled to have access, finally, to a couple of war enemies. "We could all take shifts watchin' her."

The mayor considered this for a moment, and then

shook his head. "That sounds like an awful lot of work," he said dubiously. "We'll jest have t' keep a real close eye on her without the fence. You know, be real sly-like, so they don't get suspicious that we're on to 'em. One wrong move outta either of 'em, and I'm callin' Senator McCarthy m'self. My Lord—what was Charlie thinkin'?"

After Mr. Arflot left, the mayor stood up and looked out the window at the gray autumn sky. First the visit of Eunice Grimes, and now this! Just what in Sam Hill did God have in mind for Rusty Nail? Feeling uneasy, Mayor Reverend Jerry guessed that they wouldn't have to wait long to find out.

He put on his hat and walked down to Elmer's for a beer.

Several days later, Charlie's car appeared on the outskirts of Rusty Nail. By the time he drove into town, many people were peering out of their windows and standing on their front lawns, waiting for a glimpse of his new Commie wife.

They were sorely disappointed to discover that he was alone. He parked his car on the street outside his house. As Charlie walked toward his front porch, he noticed Norma Smitty huffing and puffing up the street in his direction. Tipping his hat to her, he scurried up the front stairs and closed the door behind him without a word. Of course, this set off a storm of *Did-you-see-thats* and *Well-I-nevers* and *Ain't-that-high-and-mightys*. The town switchboard nearly blew up from the volume of kitchen-to-kitchen phone calls.

And then, the very next day, another stupefying event occurred: a truck with New York license plates rumbled into town. As it chugged down Main Street, people stared at it with the dismay of those watching incoming tanks filled with enemy troops. The truck parked in front of Charlie's house, and a couple of men began unloading a few cloth-covered objects onto Charlie's lawn.

The usually unpopular Mrs. Thelma Britches, who happened to be Charlie's next-door neighbor, suddenly found herself entertaining at least ten women who'd invited themselves over to watch the spectacle from her kitchen window. The guests gripped mismatched cups of watery coffee and peered through lace curtains at the movers.

Sandy and Franny took a less covert approach to the event. On the way home from their labors at the Klompenhower pig barn, covered in mud, they stopped on the sidewalk right in front of Charlie's house to gawk.

"I guess she's comin' pretty soon," Sandy said. "And I'm willin' to bet she's not a spy after all. I mean, what would a spy spy on here—the farmers milkin' the cows? Let's go look at her stuff." She ambled toward one of the shrouded objects.

"Hey! Get yer dirty paws off those things, kid," one of the movers called menacingly from the porch.

"Have you met her?" Sandy yelled back, pressing her luck. "The woman whose stuff this is?"

The mover stalked back to the truck and yanked out a big cardboard box. " 'Course I met her. We picked up all this stuff from 'er place in New Yawk. Had to do it in the middle of the night, for some reason. Guess she works during the day or somethin'." He started walking toward the house with the box.

Sandy and Franny looked at each other in astonishment.

"The middle-a the night!" exclaimed Sandy. "Okay, I mighta been wrong 'bout her bein' a spy. That sounds real suspicious to me." The girls plunked themselves down on the curb and watched the mover.

"Hey," Franny called to the mover, pointing to the oddly shaped items on the lawn. "What're those things?"

"I dunno," the mover shouted over his shoulder. "Looks like a buncha instrument cases or somethin'. You know, the musical kind. Touch 'em and I'll box yer ears—both-a-ya!"

Franny sat there, bemused. "Why would a spy need instruments?" she asked.

"Maybe the cases are carryin' nuclear parts instead of violins," Sandy suggested excitedly. "Safer transport—you know, like in the movies. It's like puttin' money into a mattress, where no one thinks to look for it. Boy, are things gonna get interestin' out here now."

At that moment, both movers came out of the house and climbed back into the truck. They wheeled a huge covered object to the edge of the truck's cavern and heaved it out with tremendous care. When they finally set the object on the ground, Franny heard a familiar twang and tingling noise and suddenly knew that she was seeing her first grand piano. Even Nancy Orilee's piano was an old upright.

"Look at that!" she said to Sandy, pointing at the piano's black legs. Its enormous body was covered with thick blankets and wrapped in heavy tape. "A real grand piano, like the one in the White House newsreel—you know, the one with the kid who played for the president!" Her heart pounded with excitement.

"Wow," said Sandy. "I bet you could get a mother lode of nuclear parts into that baby. We're *definitely* gonna have to come back the second she gets here. But we'll have to do it at night, you know."

"Why—so she can't see us?" Franny asked distractedly.

"Well, yeah—but also so *they* can't," Sandy said, pointing toward Thelma Britches' kitchen window. All of the usual suspects from the Sunday Colosseum peered out nosily.

Franny shook her head in disbelief. "They're worse than we are," she said. "Let's never be like that when we grow up."

"Deal," said Sandy, spitting on her palm and sticking it out for Franny to shake. Franny did the same.

When the last box had been lugged into the house, the girls walked back to Main Street. On the way, they planned their nighttime stakeout of Rusty Nail's Russian spy.

Chapter Seven

The days dragged by, and Charlie's wife still didn't bother to show up. The women of Rusty Nail nearly went crazy as they waited for the Russian to arrive.

"Well, talk about bad manners," Norma Smitty sneered a week later, holding court as usual in the Colosseum. "Remind me never to invite Mizz Russia to a party, if she's gonna be this late to things."

Then Mrs. Charity Engebraten chimed in: "You know, we better hire a guard to look over this church, in case she gets any ideas 'bout burnin' it down or anything."

"I sure hope she knows how to cut and curl her own hair, 'cause I ain't lettin' her near the Beauty Station," said Melba ferociously.

"Well, I'm not gonna jest sit by and do nothin' while

some Commie sets up shop in our town," announced Norma. "I'm gonna be startin' a club, right here in the church, unitin' the ladies of Rusty Nail against the Commie Threat. I ain't thought of a name yet, but it'll be somethin' good—jest you all wait."

And then the most unusual event took place, one that began a very significant era in Rusty Nail's history.

Up to this point, Lorraine had been standing to the side of the crowd, sipping her coffee and watching quietly. But with Norma's latest pronouncement, she suddenly straightened up.

"Now, just a minute," she said. "Don't you think that you're going a little bit too far? You all don't know a thing about this lady—I mean, besides the gossip. And, Norma, you're hardly a perfectionist when it comes to getting the facts right all the time."

Shocked silence filled the room. Franny stared at her mother, who was usually as mild as milk during these discussions.

Norma Smitty cleared her throat. "And jest what do you mean by that, Lorraine?"

"What I mean," said Lorraine, setting down her cup, "is that there're two sides to every story. She might be Russian, but does that mean that she's a spying Communist?"

Franny tugged her mother's sleeve. "Aren't they the same thing?" she whispered to her mother noisily.

"Amen to that," someone said in the back of the room.

"Not necessarily," said Lorraine. "And that's my point. I've been thinking about this a lot since last week. You all talk about Rusty Nail being all-American. But being all-American means that all folks here are innocent until proven guilty. And it also means being hospitable to strangers, and this community seems to have forgotten how to be neighborly all of a sudden."

"W-w-well . . . um, yes," stammered Mrs. Engebraten, trying to smooth over the awkwardness. "Lorraine, honey, of *course* we're going to show her every consideration when she arrives. We're just all, uh, *disappointed* that she's not here yet. But we'll give her a big Rusty Nail welcome when she shows up, won't we, ladies?"

There was another uncomfortable silence, and someone muttered, "Over my dead body" under her breath.

Franny's heart actually skipped a beat. Lorraine stared hard at Norma while the rest of the women looked at their feet with great interest. And then, to the congregation's relief, somebody changed the subject to the upcoming annual Halloween pageant at the Polk School.

As they walked home later, Franny tugged on Lorraine's sleeve again. Lorraine's little speech had stunned her. Why on *earth* was her own mother sticking up for the Russian?

"Mom," she said. "Why'd you take the Commie's side back there in the Colosseum?"

"Stop calling it that," Lorraine snapped. "It's the church, not the Colosseum." She marched a little faster, and Franny scrambled to catch up.

"Okay, well, why did you stick up for the Commie at church, then?" Franny asked pestily.

Lorraine stopped and put her hands on her hips, staring down at her daughter.

"Franny, don't say *Commie*—you sound like a politician," she said. "I meant what I said back there. I just think that that sort of behavior is, well, un-Christian and un-American."

"Why?" Franny asked. "If that woman's a spy, aren't we supposed to protect Rusty Nail from her?"

Lorraine sighed. "I don't want to ruin all of your and Sandy's fun, but I really doubt that Charlie's wife is going to be a spy," she said. "People like us have to take the high road. One of the things that makes Russia so bad is that they just throw people in jail without giving them trials. Now, we can't act the same way, or we'll be no better than they are. Do you see?"

"No one said anything about putting her in jail," said Franny, confused. "Melba just said that she wouldn't do the lady's hair, that's all." She thought for a minute. "Which is probably a good thing, not a punishment."

Lorraine smiled her sideways smile. "That's true,

sweetheart," she said. "Now let's go home and get some lunch.

"And just remember," she added as they walked down Main Street, "that not everything is always as it seems at first."

At last, the big moment arrived.

Franny and her family were finishing up supper when the news reached the Hansen household that Rusty Nail's newest resident had come. Mrs. Charity Engebraten called Lorraine and gave her a full report. After Lorraine hung up, the phone rang again almost immediately.

"Hello?" said Franny. The receiver was still warm from her mother's ear.

"It's time," said a grave, urgent voice on the other end. It was Sandy, disguising her voice for some reason. "Put Plan A into action."

"Right," said Franny excitedly, and hung up.

It was time to spy on the spy.

But first, she had to get out of the house without raising any suspicion about the nature of her mission—especially after her mother's lecture to her on the street that afternoon.

Franny drummed her fingers on the counter until an idea came to her. Then she opened the kitchen cabinet that held her mother's jumbled collection of Tupperware containers and rummaged around until she found an empty jelly jar with a lid. Using a scissors like a dagger, she jabbed several holes in the top.

She marched into the living room, where her mother was knitting and her father was listening to a rerun of the Benny Goodman jazz show on the radio. Her brothers were in their room, doing homework. A swing band played in the background as a woman sang:

> *There'll be a change in the weather,*
> *a change in the sea.*
> *Before long there'll be a change in me.*
> *My walk will be diff'rent, my talk*
> *and my name.*
> *Ain't nothin' about me is gonna be*
> *the same.*

"Man, those guys can *play*," said Franny's dad, clapping his hands on his knees in time to the music. "Listen to Benny play that clarinet. He sure can swing."

"I need to go meet Sandy in the churchyard," Franny announced.

Her parents looked up at her.

"Why in heavens do you need to meet Sandy Anne Hellickson in the churchyard on a school night?" Lorraine asked, putting down her knitting needles.

"We have to catch some fireflies," Franny answered.

"For a science project. Everyone in the class has to catch and study a different insect. Me and Sandy are supposed to bring fireflies to school tomorrow." She held out the jar as evidence. "See—we'll put them in here."

"First of all, it's *Sandy and I*," Lorraine corrected her. She looked skeptical. "And secondly, why can't Sandy just catch them at her house? There must be swarms of fireflies out at the farm."

Franny nearly panicked. She hadn't anticipated this question. "She says there aren't any out there," she said somewhat lamely. Then, more bravely, she added: "Anyway, we're supposed to do it *together*, and she said she'd rather come into town than do it at home."

Lorraine looked unconvinced, but Wes seemed eager to get back to his radio show.

"All right, but no monkey business," he said. "You're still grounded, you know," he called after Franny as she scrambled across the room toward the front door. The song continued in the background:

> *They say don't change the old for*
> *the new,*
> *But I've found out this will never do.*
> *When you grow old, you don't last*
> *long.*
> *You're here today and then*
> *tomorrow you're gone. . . .*

Franny heard her dad say: "Now, that's God's truth if I've ever heard it," and then the front door closed behind her.

The sun sank behind the cornfields, washing the world in a purple gray light and matting out the hard edges of the storefronts and houses.

Franny ran down Main Street toward the church. When she got there, she sat on the church's back steps and waited for Sandy to bike into town from her farm. Once in a while, she heard the tattered old screen door to Elmer's Bar flap open and slap shut, but otherwise, the town center was quiet and still. Not even the mildest breeze fluttered the leaves on the trees.

Suddenly someone grabbed Franny's shoulder. "Boo!" a voice behind her screamed.

Franny shrieked, her heart pounding in her chest, but it was just Sandy, dressed all in black like a burglar. She was clearly pleased with her ambush, but her grin melted away as she looked Franny up and down.

"Jeez, Franny," she said, smacking her forehead with her hand. "I said Plan *A*—didn't you hear me?"

"Of course I heard you," said Franny, not yet over her scare. "I'm here, aren't I?"

Sandy scowled. "Okay, so you got here in time. Big deal. But what was the *second* part of Plan A?" she asked Socratically. "Hmm, I seem to remember sayin' somethin' about *wearin' dark clothing* so no one could see us. You might as well be wearin' a mess of blinkin' Christmas lights."

Franny looked down at her outfit and her heart sank. Sandy was right: her white shirt and red pants were anything but stealth.

"I could go back and change," she offered.

Sandy gave an exasperated sigh. "It's too late—ole Wes and Lorraine'll know we're up to somethin' then for sure. Let's go."

The girls set out for Charlie's house, cutting across backyards, climbing fences, and hiding in bushes along the way. When they finally got there, they snuck around to the far side and wedged themselves between an unwieldy peony bush and the wall of the house—just below the front-parlor window. It was balmy for October, and the window had been left open to let in the evening breezes.

"What's this one?" said Charlie's voice from inside. It sounded like he was unsnapping the clasp of a case.

"That is the viola," said a woman's voice laced with a thrilling accent. "It was one of the finer pieces my father ever made."

"And this one?" said Charlie.

"Oh, that was his favorite violin," the woman said. "The famous violinist Isaac Stern once borrowed it for a concert. It has the purest tone."

"I can never tell the difference between a viola and a

violin," said Charlie. "I swear, Olga—I had no idea you were going to move a whole orchestra into my house."

Sandy leaned in toward Franny. "We hit the jackpot," she whispered excitedly. "I bet she has long black hair and wears a cape and those boots with fur around their tops."

Franny shook her head. "She's a spy, not a superhero," she scoffed.

From inside, the woman said: "Well, I have never traveled with fewer than three or four trunks. It's in my nature, I suppose—even under these circumstances. And, anyway, I had to bring all of these with me. The New York Philharmonic, or someone worse, would have confiscated them all if I had left them in my apartment in the city."

"I'm gonna look," Sandy whispered boldly to Franny. "Here I go." Moving as slowly as an inchworm, she peeked up over the windowsill. The yellow light from inside bathed her damp forehead. After what seemed like an eternity, she dove down into the bush again to report back to Franny.

"Well, I'll be a monkey's uncle," she said.

"What?" whispered Franny urgently.

"She looks just like we thought she would," Sandy said, looking somewhat dazed. "Kinda like the Russians you see in the movies, with long black hair. Go on and see for yourself."

"I'm scared they'll see me," Franny said, feeling Jell-O–y inside all of a sudden.

Sandy sighed in exasperation. "They're not even payin' attention. They're just pullin' instruments out of boxes—nothin' top-secret. I guess she already took all of the nuclear parts out of the cases before Charlie got a look at them. Now go on and look, fraidy-cat."

Then they realized that the room above was silent, and Franny's heart skipped a beat. Had they been overheard? The girls held their breath, and to their relief, the conversation in the parlor began again.

"It's getting late," Franny said, stalling. "I'm going home. I don't want to get grounded even longer."

"Chicken," taunted Sandy. "*Bok, bok, bok. Girlie* chicken. Even Gretchen Beasley would look, and you're too sca-a-ared."

Franny could only tolerate so much of this. She gave Sandy a little shove and timidly peered into the room. Charlie Koenig sat in a chair surrounded by a terrain of torn-open cardboard boxes and glistening instruments perched on stands amidst the mess. In the corner of the room stood the spectacular grand piano Franny had seen on the lawn. Its magnificent lacquered curves gleamed in the light and reflected the movements of Charlie and the Russian spy. Even seeing the woman's reflection gave Franny a little jolt. She was laying eyes on a real live "Commie" for the first time in her life!

The spy, for her part, apparently oblivious to the sensation she was causing outside, dug around in another box in the far corner of the room, out of Franny's view. From the reflection in the piano, she appeared tall and slender, with a long black cord of a braid running down her back. She pulled an object out of the box and said to Charlie: "And this is one of my favorite instruments of all. Would you like to see how it works?"

"Sure," said Charlie, laughing.

Franny squinted at the reflection in the piano, trying to make out what the object was. The woman's footsteps clicked toward the window.

Suddenly, out of nowhere, something smacked Franny right on the nose. She let out a shocked squawk and fell back into the peony bush, covering her face with her hands.

The woman leaned out the window and looked directly down at the girls, who were paralyzed by the humiliation of getting caught. The yellow light behind the Russian cast a halo around her head and outlined the edges of her sharp cheekbones. She said over her shoulder to Charlie: "How do you call this in English?"

In her left hand, she brandished the item with which she had whacked Franny.

"It's called a flyswatter," said Charlie, joining her at the window.

"Yes," the woman said. "Very good at getting rid of household pests." And she looked straight at Franny and Sandy again.

"Sandy Anne Hellickson and Franny Hansen." Charlie smirked down at the girls. "What a surprise. This is Olga. Olga, meet the town's most notorious troublemakers."

"Howdy-do," said Sandy. Franny mumbled a salutation from behind her hands.

"Franny here is quite a musician in her own right," Charlie informed Olga. "I hear that she gave a fine piano performance for an important government official not too long ago."

"Is that so," said Olga, looking only mildly interested. "Did you notice my piano?"

Franny nodded, her nose red from the flyswatter and her cheeks burning with embarrassment.

"Well, I might have let you play it," Olga said. "If you had not spied on us like a nasty little goblin."

"What happened to your thumb, Franny?" Charlie asked, looking at the dirty bandage covering her bruised thumb.

"We've been fixing Mr. Klompenhower's pig barn," Sandy explained, standing on her tiptoes and trying to see into the room again. "She whacked her finger real hard with a hammer."

"A *pig* barn," Olga said, as though she had never heard of something so disgusting. "How quaint." She ducked back inside.

"Sounds like a hard way to earn pocket cash," Charlie said, still wearing an amused look. "Go on home now, girls. And next time you want to stop by, use the front door, not the window."

He withdrew back into the parlor.

"Wait!" said Franny. "Do you need any handiwork around the house?"

"What are you *doin*'?" hissed Sandy. "We haven't even finished the pig barn and you want to get us *more* work?"

"Shh—I have a plan," whispered Franny. She turned back to Charlie, who poked his head back out the window. "Sandy and I need to earn money to pay the mayor back. We ruined his car and have to pay his bill to get it fixed."

"How'd you do that?" Charlie asked, looking amazed.

"We hit it by accident with a water balloon, and he drove it into Mr. Klompenhower's chicken cart," Franny explained. "Our parents told us that we need to do jobs around town to earn back the money. So, do you need anything done?"

"I can't think of anything off the top of my head," Charlie said.

"Well, I noticed that your porch needs a new coat of paint—how 'bout that?" Franny offered.

"Oh, *man*," said Sandy under her breath. "This better be a good plan."

"It does?" Charlie asked hesitantly. "Well, I guess it *has* been a while since I painted it."

"We'd do a really good job," Franny pressed.

"Well, okay," said Charlie. "But on one condition: no more spying. How does five dollars each sound?"

"Done, and done," Franny said. "We'll come on Saturday."

The girls retreated to the bushes behind Thelma Britches' house.

"All right," Sandy fumed. "What's your plan, genius?"

"Look," said Franny. "We have to earn back that money anyway. Not only will we knock ten dollars off our bill, but we can also spy on the Russian—right from her own front porch! See? It's perfect." In addition, she secretly wanted to get near that piano again—but she didn't mention that to Sandy.

"Hmph," scowled Sandy, kicking at the ground. "I'd still rather spy from behind a bush than from a porch with a paintbrush in my hand, but I guess you're right."

The girls walked back to Main Street on the town's sidewalks this time. At the last minute, Franny remembered that she was supposed to return with a jar full of fireflies. But by then, it was so late that she and Sandy had to make do with scraping some ants and dirt into the jar instead. Lorraine made her leave it outside on the sidewalk.

When Franny went to sleep later that night, she dreamt about a huge jelly jar filled with shining instruments. Olga held it in her hands and offered it to Franny. It looked so heavy and breakable that Franny was afraid to take it, but Olga insisted.

Just as Franny reached out to take the jar, she woke up—her arms stretched into the air.

Chapter Eight

The girls worked at the Klompenhower farm after school every day that week. Sandy spent most of the time dawdling around and eating her stale candy. When it came to making mischief, Sandy had all the energy in the world, but chores always brought out her lazy side.

But at long last, the girls drove the final nail into the wall of the pig barn. They stepped back to admire their handiwork.

"Somethin's not quite right about it," Sandy said.

"What are you talking about?" asked Franny. "It's perfect. There's barely any space between the boards."

Sandy stared at the wall for a minute and thought hard.

"That's it!" she said suddenly, and reached for her

hammer. She started wrenching the nails out of one of the planks.

"What are you doing?" shrieked Franny. "It took me forever to get that one straight."

"That's just the thing," explained Sandy as she pulled the board loose. "It's *too* perfect. If we do that good a job, everyone in town will find a reason to make us come and do their work for them, even when we're done earnin' back that money. We have to make the wall look *okay* but not *great*. Get it?"

Sandy had a point, so Franny helped her pry the board loose. Then they nailed it back on slightly crooked, and surveyed the final result with satisfaction.

Then, the next day, they trudged off in the direction of Charlie Koenig's house to paint his front porch. To the girls' disappointment, Charlie answered the front door instead of Olga.

"Hi, ladies," he said through the screen door. "Want some sandwiches before you start?"

"Can we eat them inside?" Sandy asked in a very forward manner. She craned her neck to see the foyer behind Charlie.

"Sure," said Charlie pleasantly. "Come on into the kitchen."

Sandy practically tore the screen door off its hinges and ran into the house, and Franny followed tentatively. Stacks of boxes lined the walls, and packing paper littered the floor. Propped up against one of the walls stood an unusual painting of a saint. The shiny gold background glinted in the sunlight streaming through the window.

"Wow!" said Sandy, inspecting the picture. "Is that real gold? Like they put in fillings in your teeth?"

"Don't touch that," commanded a voice from the top of the stairs. "It is a Russian icon, and worth more than a hundred silly pig barns."

The girls looked up in surprise. Even though it was past noon, Olga stood there wearing a long silk robe, her black hair loose around her shoulders. In the daylight, Franny could see that the Russian was indeed very pretty—but not in a warm, welcoming way. Her strong face could have been chiseled on a totem pole, and her dark eyes glittered like onyx.

"Just so you know: I keep a flyswatter in every room, *Dyevushka*," the lady added for good measure. "And you have seen already how fast I am with it." She marched back into her bedroom.

"The kitchen's this way, Sandy," said Charlie.

"What'd she just call me?" Sandy asked as Charlie shoveled the girls into the kitchen. "Was that a dirty word in Russian? Wow."

"Don't get too excited," Charlie said. "It only means *girl*."

The girls ate peanut butter sandwiches and drank farm milk from big mason jars. When they finished, Charlie gave them paintbrushes and sent them off to the front porch. Several cans of sticky white paint stood next to the door.

"Give it the first coat today and we'll do another tomorrow," he said cheerfully. He walked back inside and closed the front door, blocking their view into the house.

Sandy glared at Franny and put her hands on her hips.

"Nice job, Franny," she said. "This place is like a fortress. What's the point of bein' here if we can't even get a look inside?" She sulkily plunged her brush into one of the paint cans.

Franny had to admit that her campaign to spy on the Russian didn't look very promising. In fact, they didn't see a hint of her for the rest of the day, and the front door stayed firmly shut. Sandy snuck around the side of the house at one point, but Charlie caught sight of her peering through the parlor window and abruptly pulled down the shade.

"Wow—we sure are gettin' a lot of spyin' done," Sandy said sarcastically. "I'm real glad that we took this job."

Franny sighed. The girls painted in silence for the rest of the afternoon. And, of course, they made sure to leave spatters here and there, in the spirit of doing an okay-but-not-great job.

The next morning, before church, the Hansens' phone rang. Owen answered.

"Franny, it's for you," he said, dropping the receiver rudely on the floor. "It's just Scrappy," which was his nickname for Sandy.

Franny picked up the receiver. "Hello?"

The caller gave a feeble cough on the other end of the line. "Franny?" said a weak voice. "Is that you? Can you hear me?" This was followed by another cough.

Franny rolled her eyes. "Hi, Sandy," she said.

"This might be the last time I ever talk to you," Sandy moaned and wheezed dramatically. "I'm horribly sick— probably dyin'. I think it's pneumonia. Daddy's even lettin' me stay home from church—that's how bad it is."

"Oh, *really*," said Franny, examining a little scratch on the toe of her shoe.

"Yes, really," rasped Sandy. "D'ya think you can finish the porch without me this afternoon?"

Franny gave an exasperated sigh.

"I'll try and come later," Sandy added pitifully. "If I can crawl out of bed onto my bike. Hopefully, my legs'll work. I'm so weak I can hardly hold the phone."

"Fine," snapped Franny. "I'll do the porch. But you owe me a *huge* favor."

"Thanks, old pal," said Sandy, suddenly sounding remarkably chipper, and she hung up.

After Mayor Reverend Jerry's sermon, Franny walked

over to Charlie's house alone. The first coat of paint on the porch had dried overnight. She rang the doorbell.

To Franny's enormous surprise, the Russian opened the door.

"Yes?" she said formally, looking down at Franny.

"U-u-uh," stuttered Franny nervously. "I'm just here to finish painting the porch."

"All right," said Olga, yawning. She wore the same lovely silk robe she'd been wearing the day before, and something about her suggested a warm, luxuriant morning nap. "Knock when you are finished," she said, and she began to shut the front door.

"The paint and brushes are in the foyer," Franny said quickly.

"Oh," said Olga. "Come in and get them."

"Thanks, Mrs. Koenig," she said, reaching for the screen door.

"My name is *not* Koenig," Olga snapped. "It is Malenkov. Madame Malenkov to you, *Dyevushka*."

"Oh," said Franny. "But I thought you were married to Charlie."

The Russian looked perplexed for a minute and tapped her fingers on her lips. And then she said: "Come in and get the paint if you want it."

Franny scurried inside and gathered up the supplies as Olga drifted off into the kitchen. Franny went back out onto the porch. She daringly left the front door open and closed only the screen door, thus providing herself with a clear view into the house. Beginning with the banisters, she began coating the porch with a second layer of white paint.

Soon she heard soothing kitchen noises coming from the back of the house: a teakettle whistling, water rushing quietly in a sink, the clink of silverware on a plate. Then, after a little while, there was a flutter of silk, and Olga swept through the hallway and into the parlor, where Franny had first seen her.

Franny crawled over to the parlor window and, on her knees, painted the section of porch below the window. From inside, she heard the familiar creak of the lid above the piano keys being lifted. Olga began to play scales to warm up her fingers. Up and down four octaves she went, and even this basic exercise sounded thrilling to Franny.

Suddenly the scales stopped, and Olga began to play a piece that Franny had never heard before. It was captivating, and as Franny listened, she could visualize the notes of the melody. She stopped painting and sat down beneath the window. After a few minutes, she peeked over the sill, just as she and Sandy had done a week earlier.

Olga's back faced the porch. Her fingers glided over the keys, and she bowed and raised her head dramatically as she played. Franny stared at the pianist's fingers and noted with surprise that the artist's hands were as large and inelegant as those of any farmer from Rusty Nail.

Olga stopped playing to turn a page of the music. Then she froze and dropped her hands to the keyboard.

"I know that you are watching me, *Dyevushka*," she said.

Franny's face burned with embarrassment. "How could you tell?"

Olga turned around. "Because I have eyes in the back of my head," she said, narrowing the eyes in the front of her head.

"I wasn't trying to spy; I was just listening," Franny tried to explain. Big fat baby tears welled in the corners of her eyes. She was suddenly very glad that Sandy wasn't there.

Olga still glared at her. "It seems that you like to spy a good deal. Every time I come downstairs, I expect to see two beady little eyes looking at me through the windows."

Franny swallowed. "I'm sorry, Madame Mackelov, but—"

"Malenkov!" Olga interrupted sharply.

"Malenkov," Franny repeated, her face reddening even more. "It's just that . . . I've just never seen anyone really good play the piano before." And then, to her humiliation, a big tear ran down the side of her nose.

Olga stared at her. Franny thought that the Russian was going to reprimand her some more, but instead, the woman said: "Well, you will be glad to know that this is not the first time my Rachmaninoff has brought someone to tears. I am glad that I have not lost my touch."

Franny quickly wiped away her tear. "It's the first time that your *what* has made someone cry?" she asked.

"My *Rachmaninoff*," Olga said, pronouncing the name with great Russian gusto, emphasizing every syllable. "The famous composer. Why have you not heard of him? I thought that Charles said that you are a pianist of the highest stature."

"I don't know," Franny said dully. "I guess my old teacher just never taught me him."

"Even if she had, you probably could not have played his music," Olga said haughtily. "Very few women can. Their hands are too small. You need wide, wonderful hands to play Rachmaninoff's beautiful work. Let me see yours."

Franny held her paint-spattered hands up in front of the window. Olga came over to inspect them through the screen.

"Well," she said after a moment. "They are good hands after all. Very wide for a girl. You will either be a very good pianist or, more likely, a very good farm wife. I hope you have a good teacher." She strode back to her piano.

A farm wife! This woman had a lot of nerve. "I don't have a teacher anymore!" Franny shouted. "So I guess I'll just have to be a farmer, 'cause there's no one left in this dumb town to teach me." The tears threatened to return, and she bent down and started painting again so that Olga couldn't see her face.

The Russian didn't say anything. She just turned back to the keyboard and started playing. Not a beautiful piece this time but a wild piece, filled with trickery and teasing. Franny painted the porch floor with hard, swift strokes.

She worked long after Olga stopped playing and left the music room. Charlie came home and complimented her work, but she barely heard him. When she was done, Franny cupped her hands around her mouth and called up at the house: "I'm done!"

No response—not even a flicker of a curtain. In a foul mood, Franny stuffed her hands into her pockets and stalked back home.

That night, Franny's noisy thoughts kept her awake. She tossed and turned in her bed and thought nasty thoughts about the Russian. Everyone had been right: Commies were just mean, haughty people, and now Franny could see why people in America hated them so much.

But as the heavy, maize-colored moon rose in the big sky outside Franny's window, she kept thinking about what Sandy had said to her at the Klompenhower farm: *I mean, you're real good at the piano and all, but maybe it's not meant to be or somethin'.*

And every time Franny heard this in her mind, she scowled and kicked at her covers. Defiance swelled in her and then died down and then swelled again, like water boiling and subsiding in a pot over and over again.

Then an impossible black thought crossed her mind: maybe she should try to convince Olga to be her new piano teacher.

Her stomach prickled as she pondered the possibility: What would the women at the Colosseum say? Would they all think that she was in cahoots with the spy? Not to mention that Olga herself was terrifying! Just being around her made Franny feel jittery and like she was doing something wrong, but wasn't that what Franny's dad meant by "going to the crossroads"? After his Duke Ellington tale, Wes's next favorite story was about Robert Johnson, a blues musician who'd gone once to a certain crossroads in Mississippi. According to the legend, there he met up with the devil and sold him his soul. In exchange, the devil made him a master at the guitar.

Now that Franny thought about it, Olga lived at a crossroads too: Charlie's house sat on the corner of Oak Street and Fair Street. This fact seemed like no coincidence. Olga's appearance seemed nothing short of a dark miracle. And then Sandy had been talking about signs the other day. Wasn't this as strong a sign as any?

Finally, at about three a.m., an exhausted Franny resolved to go back to Olga's house that week and secretly ask the lady to teach her. Something in her gut told her that she *had* to do it.

After all, people in Rusty Nail usually didn't get second chances. If Franny was the rare exception, she'd better take advantage of it.

Chapter Nine

Nearly a week passed before Franny got up the nerve to approach Olga. Four days in a row, she left the Polk School and walked toward the Russian's house, only to have her courage falter once the house came into sight. And each day when she got back to Main Street, Franny loitered in front of Charlie's office, hoping that the woman would come by. She did not.

In fact, the Russian didn't make a single appearance in town, which of course made the townspeople even madder. Not only was Olga a Commie, everyone mumbled, but she was an *uppity* Commie! It was just Rusty Nail's luck to land a snotty Russian.

Finally, on Friday, Franny forced herself to march up

the freshly painted porch stairs and ring the bell. A few minutes passed.

"Yes?" said Olga's voice at last. She didn't even bother to open the door a crack.

"It's Franny, Madame Malenkov," said Franny, her voice quavering.

"Who?" said the voice, with a trace of irritation.

Franny swallowed. "Frances Hansen," she said. "I painted your porch."

Silence.

"You know, the spy," Franny added somewhat desperately.

Olga opened the door and looked down at her stiffly. "*Now* what do you want?" she said.

"U-u-uh," Franny stammered. "I just, um, wanted to know if you needed anything else done around the house."

"No," Olga answered, starting to close the door. She winced in pain, and Franny saw that she was wearing a back brace. "Charles will let you know if we do."

"Wait!" said Franny, knowing that a fully closed door meant that she had failed completely. "I mean, I can do anything. I can build things, and clean too. That sort of thing." *Ugh!* she thought. *If Sandy heard me actually asking for more work, I'd never hear the end of it!*

Olga closed the door without another word.

There was nothing left for Franny to do but go home

and fume. But, of course, being told no only made her more determined.

And so, the next afternoon, she went back to the crossroads. This time Olga slammed the door shut without even saying a word.

Franny refused to give in. The very next day, she walked yet *again* to the Russian's house.

This time Olga opened the door before Franny even reached out to ring the doorbell.

"I think that I know what you want, *Dyevushka*," she declared before Franny could say anything. "You do not seem like a good-Samaritan type who does housework without expecting something in return. So, listen to me: I do *not* teach the piano to beginners."

"I'm *not* a beginner!" yelled Franny. "And my name is Franny, not Dee-ev-oosh-ka, or whatever you keep saying. And if you don't give me lessons, no one will. I'll go to waste, and it will be your fault."

Olga pursed her lips in disapproval. "Do you not *know* who I am?" she thundered. "I am a great performer, *Dyevushka*, not a common teacher who gives away lessons like at a charity."

Franny scowled. "Well, who are you performing for here in Rusty Nail? You haven't even left your house yet! And I'm not looking for charity. I'll work for my lessons— like I told you. Please?"

"The answer is no, no, and no again," Olga said. "I have enough problems in my life right now without a meddlesome girl making demands on me." And then, as she started to close the door, she yelled, "Ohhh!" and grabbed at her back brace.

"What happened to your back?" Franny asked nosily.

"I hurt it lifting one of those boxes," Olga moaned. "Now go away, girl."

Franny gave one last plea before the door closed. "Please give me a chance!" she exclaimed. "I was born to play the piano—everyone says so!"

Olga opened the door again and glared at her. "Let me ask you a question, *Dyevushka*," she said.

"Okay," said Franny warily.

"If something happened to your hands tomorrow, and you couldn't play the piano ever again—would you die?"

Franny blinked. Was this some sort of trick question? She racked her mind. What did people need to live? Water, food, a house. She couldn't imagine a Red Cross survival kit containing a piano.

"I don't think so," she ventured.

"Aha!" exclaimed Olga triumphantly. "You see? Then you weren't born to play the piano after all. For real pianists, playing is not a hobby—it's the very basis of their lives and souls, and they have no choice: play or die. Now leave me *alone*."

And she slammed the door.

★ ★ ★

A few days later, Sandy and Franny played an after-school game of marbles on the sidewalk in front of Wes's Main Street office. Franny had won all but two of Sandy's marbles, and she aimed at a big blue one just inside the chalk circle they'd drawn on the ground.

"You'd better not take Old Blue," Sandy growled. "It took me fifty-three games to win that from Lowell." Lowell was her fifteen-year-old brother, and he was the town's expert marbles player.

Franny flicked her marble into the ring and hit Old Blue with a satisfying *clack*.

"To the victor go the spoils," she said, using a phrase she'd learned in history class that week. She reached into the ring and snatched the marble out.

"Hey-y-y!" shouted Sandy. "No fair! Your hand was way inside the line." They argued until someone behind them said:

"No brawling on the sidewalk, girls. It's just not lady-like."

They turned around and saw Charlie Koenig standing over them, holding several big bags of groceries and packages from the butcher.

"Why're you carryin' all those bags?" Sandy asked, shielding her eyes from the late-afternoon sun. "Isn't your fancy wife supposed to do all the shoppin' for you now?"

Charlie laughed. "She's not feeling so well right now," he answered. "And I'm going out of town on a case for a week or two. So I figured that I'd stock up for her before I left."

"And I bet she makes you wear her apron 'round the house too, huh, Charlie?" Sandy said.

Charlie reached into a bag, pulled out an apple, and bounced it right off the top of Sandy's head.

"Boy, you're sassy, Sandy Anne," he said, smirking, and he walked toward his house on Oak Street.

The girls watched him go.

"Why doesn't that woman just come out of her house already?" Sandy said, picking up the apple and dusting it off on her sleeve. "It's not like there's a firin' squad waitin' for her. Not a real one, anyway."

Franny wasn't listening. *So, Charlie's going out of town,* she thought. That gave her *just* the idea she was looking for.

Pleased, she picked up a marble, shot it into the circle, and took Sandy's last marble as victor's loot.

Chapter Ten

The next morning, Charlie drove out of town in his mint green Ford sedan. Olga drew all of the curtains across the windows of their house and hunkered down in her fortress.

Several blocks away, Franny secretly plotted her strategy. She let three days pass, then four, and decided that day five of Charlie's absence would be the right time to strike.

That day, after school, she strode to the Russian's house. She rang the doorbell three times before Olga answered.

"Oh, for the love of God—*now* what?" she said when she saw Franny standing there. A huge heap of moving boxes still cluttered the foyer, and packing paper littered the floor.

"Charlie told me to come by to see if you needed anything," Franny lied boldly. "He said you were sick."

"I am *not* sick," Olga said peevishly. "I hurt my back, that's all. I do not need anything."

"Are you sure?" Franny pressed. "It sure looks to me like you need some help cleaning up in there. Charlie *said* to help you, and he'll be mad at me if you make me go away again."

"He said that?" Olga asked suspiciously.

"He said he'd make me paint the whole outside of the house," Franny persisted. "And then you'd have to have me around all the time."

"I suppose I would not mind some help cleaning up the kitchen," Olga conceded, looking as though she'd just been defeated at chess. "And I need some fresh milk too. All right—come in, *Dyevushka*."

Franny scrambled into the house. Piles of dirty dishes covered the counter near the sink. The Russian lay on a couch in the living room while Franny started tidying up. When she finished washing the counters, she ran out to Hans Zimmerman's grocery store and got several bottles of milk, which she placed neatly in Olga's refrigerator.

"Madame Malenkov—I'm done," Franny said, peeking into the living room. Olga lay there, the back of her hand on her forehead like a tragic silent-film star. "Do you want to see what a good job I did?"

Olga heaved herself off the sofa and staggered into the

kitchen. "Very good," she said. "Thank you." She reached for her purse and handed Franny a dollar.

"Thank you, but I don't need your dollar," Franny said humbly. "I'll tell you what, though. I'll come back and help you every day that Charlie's gone if you just give me one little piano lesson. Just think about it—all that help, and all you'd have to do is sit there and listen to me play for half an hour. And if you think that I'm good enough to teach some more, I'll help you after he gets back in exchange for lessons." Her own boldness shocked her, but the words kept coming out anyway.

Olga looked like she might cry from frustration. "How many times do I have to tell you, *Dyevushka*? No, no, no, *no*. Do you not speak English? In that case: *Nyet! Non! Nein! Nie!*"

"*Please?*" Franny pleaded. "Just one lesson, and if you don't think I'm good enough, I'll never ask you again. And I'll still help you until Charlie comes back anyway. Either way, you win—see?"

Olga looked like she was really going to let Franny have it, but instead she got up and limped into the foyer.

"Follow me," she said.

Franny marched triumphantly after Olga into the music room. The Russian sat on a little couch near the front window and closed her eyes, her hands on her back.

"Go sit down at the piano," she instructed.

"Aren't you going to come sit next to me?" asked

Franny over her shoulder as she sat in front of the splendid piano.

"I am not giving you a lesson," said Olga. "I want you to play your best piece for me, so I can see how much of an amateur you really are. Go ahead and begin."

Franny took a deep breath, and her hands trembled. What should she play? Olga was a dramatic person, and therefore, the situation clearly called for the most dramatic piece Franny knew. She decided to play the only Russian piece she knew, by Tchaikovsky, hoping that it would curry favor with Olga. She racked her mind to remember the notes.

"I am waiting," said Olga, tapping her foot on the floor.

Franny pretended that she was back at her apartment, practicing the piece. Slowly the jumpy haze in her busy mind cleared, and in her mind she saw the notes on the paper. She began to play, tentatively at first, and then with greater gusto. She liked what she heard, and played more showily. Remembering what Olga had looked like at the piano, Franny tried bowing and raising her head in time with the music. Her fantasy about charming a Russian with Russian music was coming true at last!

She finished the piece with great relish. Silently congratulating herself, Franny folded her hands in her lap and waited for Olga's astonished praise to wash over her.

Instead, a long silence followed. And then the Russian

said: "Your playing is melodramatic and you are utterly undisciplined. Your fingering is appalling. And your head movements are gauche. You are as primitive as I suspected."

Humiliated, Franny got up to leave. Her face burned.

"But—to my surprise, you are not beyond hope," Olga said. "Somehow, under all of that noise, you seem to have good musical instinct."

"What does that mean?" asked Franny, not knowing how to feel about anything at that point.

"It means that you have something good in your playing that cannot be taught," Olga said, and sighed. "I will make this deal with you. You must unpack all of my boxes and clean the house and do the grocery shopping and the dishes for me until Charlie gets back. If you do a good job, *then* I will give you a lesson."

"It's a deal," Franny said. She had to stop herself from reaching out to shake Olga's hand, Sandy-style.

"Just a minute, *Dyevushka,*" Olga commanded. "I want you to know that under other circumstances, you would not meet my standards, and I am making an exception now only because I need your help in the house. If you are lazy or if you disappoint me, I will not think twice about leaving you to your bad fingering."

Franny grew excited despite Olga's harsh words. "When will my first lesson be?" she asked.

"Come after school each day next week, and on Friday will be your lesson," answered Olga. "And if you annoy me in any way, or spy on me—no lesson. And that includes keeping that ragamuffin friend of yours out of the bushes as well."

This last part was a tall order, but Franny nodded gratefully. "Thank you very much," she said.

"And do not forget to tell your mother where you are each day," said Olga. "I do not want a hysterical housewife knocking on my door, thinking that a Communist has kidnapped her daughter."

So Olga knew about the rumors flying around Rusty Nail. Franny didn't know what to say to that.

"Do not just stand there like a stick of wood," Olga said. "Go home. Now I have a headache from your Tchaikovsky in addition to the pain in my back."

Franny was just about to leave when Olga called to her: "Wait! There is one more thing, *Dyevushka*. While you work here, you are never, *never* to answer the phone if it rings, do you understand?"

"What?" said Franny. "How come?"

Olga scowled. "That is not your affair. If you disobey me about this, you will not set foot in this house again."

"Okay," agreed Franny, confused. Why would Olga not want to talk to anyone? Lorraine talked on the phone for hours at a time, twirling the cord around her finger and examining her nails.

She left and sprinted all the way home, both thrilled and petrified about the deal she'd cut at the Rusty Nail crossroads. Franny could hardly believe that her plan had worked. Not only was she getting lessons from a pro, she now had keys to the fortress that no one else in Rusty Nail had been able to invade.

But first she had to tell her parents.

"So, guess what happened at football practice today," said Owen that evening at dinner, mashed potato churning around in his mouth like clothes in a washing machine.

"Don't talk with your mouth full," said Lorraine. "What happened?"

"We all ran outta the locker room and Crazy Frankie was passed out right in the middle of the field," said Jessie. "Lying there like a dead raccoon. It took three of us to haul him away, and he smelled like the bathroom over at Elmer's Bar."

"And just how do *you* know what Elmer's Bar smells like?" exclaimed Lorraine, sitting up straight as a poker.

Jessie blushed up to his hairline. "I meant, he smells what I *think* that place would smell like," he said quickly. "Jeez, Ma—I'm just trying to be creative in my story-telling."

Lorraine glared at him suspiciously as she handed the tuna casserole to Owen. Franny figured that it was as good a time as any to tell everyone her news.

"So, guess what happened to *me* today," she said as casually as possible, studying the dismal contents of her plate. "After school, I went over to Charlie's house to bring his new wife some groceries because she hurt her back and can't go shopping by herself and he's out of town and then she offered to give me a piano lesson because she's a famous pianist and all I have to do is go over there every day after school to help her unpack and stuff."

She peered meekly up to see how her announcement had gone over.

Everyone was staring at her, their forks frozen in the air halfway to their mouths, as though time had suddenly stopped. Even the radio in the living room seemed to go silent.

Wes cleared his throat. "What did you say?" he asked.

Franny sank down in her chair as though she'd drunk a shrinking potion from *Alice in Wonderland*. "Madame Malenkov's going to give me a piano lesson if I help her around the house," she said.

"Madame *what*?" shouted Jessie. "You call her 'Madame Mal-vee-koff'? You're going to work for the Commie spy? Are you *crazy*?"

"Miss Hamm is definitely rubbing off on you, isn't she," added Owen. "I'll call the loony bin and tell 'em to have a room waiting."

Wes and Lorraine looked at each other with surprise. "And just how did this come about?" asked Lorraine.

"I already *told* you," said Franny, growing indignant.

"Fran-*ces*," said Wes, staring down at her with the gravity of God and country. "You and Sandy haven't been harassing that woman in any way, have you?"

"No-o!" Franny lied. "Sandy and I were just over

there painting the porch, and Charlie told her that I play the piano too, and one thing led to another. Can I go?"

Lorraine stood up and started snatching plates off the table. "I'm not very comfortable with this arrangement," she said. "First of all, we don't even *know* this woman. I don't like the way she hasn't even come out of her house, but invites you in with open arms for some reason. It sounds fishy to me. And how much would she charge? We can't afford a fancy teacher like Nancy Orilee's parents."

"She won't charge anything," said Franny desperately. "I'd work for her in exchange for the first lesson, and if it goes well, she'll give me more. And you said yourself that it's bad to judge someone without having even met them! Isn't that what you're doing now?"

Lorraine clattered a pot down into the sink. "Hmph," she said, clearly annoyed to have been caught in a hypocritical moment. "That's only all right when I say it, but not you. I'm going to call her right now and talk this over." She marched over to the phone and dialed Charlie's number. An electrically tense silence charged the room as the family waited for Olga to answer.

"She's not picking up," said Lorraine, frowning as she hung up.

"That's 'cause she has a hurt back!" shouted Franny. "She can't get up!"

Wes stood up next to his wife. "Hold on a minute, Lorraine. Don't get so upset," he said, and Franny felt the pendulum subtly swing in the other direction. "This might be a great thing for Franny. The Russian's a famous pianist, you said? What are the odds of that? I don't see any real harm in letting her have one lesson. Who else is going to teach her?"

"I just don't think . . . ," Lorraine trailed off warily.

"I guess that old trout Smitty's gotten to you after all," Wes said. "I always thought that you were way too sensible to succumb to mass hysteria about this Commie invasion nonsense."

"No one's being hysterical," answered Lorraine. "I just don't want there to be any trouble, that's all."

Wes's eyes shone like they did when he talked about Duke Ellington. "Oh, I doubt there's going to be any trouble," he said. "The woman is Charlie's wife, after all— and don't forget that he loves Rusty Nail and everyone in it. He wouldn't have come back here after law school if he didn't. And in any case—in this place, we have to take whatever opportunities come our way, 'cause the pickings are slim."

Franny nodded piteously at her mother.

"I'll think about it, but I'm not making any promises," said Lorraine, clearly still dubious. "But I'm going to call her this week to talk things over."

"I'll take care of it," said Wes quickly. "I'll swing by her house tomorrow, introduce myself, and see what's what. I don't want you to worry about a thing." He gave his wife a peck on the cheek. Then he leaned over and ruffled Franny's hair. "Let's give it a shot," he said.

In the living room, a big-band program came on the radio.

"Oh, this is a good song—it's Count Basie!" Wes yelled. "Franny, c'mere!"

Franny leaped up from the table and ran after him into the living room. To her surprise, Wes pushed her music books off his trumpet case for the first time in many months and pulled out the shining brass instrument. Then he turned up the radio as loud as it would go, and "One O'Clock Jump" blared out of the speakers.

"You try to play along on the piano, and I'll play too," Wes shouted over the music. "One, two, three!"

He blew into his trumpet with all of his might. Franny stood in front of the keyboard and tried to play some of the chords, glancing over her shoulder at her father.

"That'sa girl!" Wes yelled, and put the trumpet to his mouth again. His cheeks swelled out like balloons as he blew. Franny tried to listen carefully and imitate the melody. The music got wilder and wilder, and they both played as hard as they could. The ruckus grew so loud that Lorraine and Owen and Jessie stuck their fingers in their ears. At last, the song thundered to an end, and Wes let out a final deafening blast. Franny leaped up and down and clapped.

From outside, Stella Brunsvold hollered up from the sidewalk below: "*Quiet* up there, Wes Hansen! Who d'ya think ya are, waking up the whole neighborhood like that?" even though it was only seven o'clock.

Flushed, Wes tossed his trumpet onto the couch and slammed the living-room window shut. He stalked over to his daughter and gave her a fierce hug.

"You might just make it after all, Mozart," he said, and squeezed her extra hard.

Chapter Eleven

The next afternoon, right after school, Franny ran straight home. But instead of going upstairs to her apartment, she burst into her father's accounting office on the ground floor.

Her father sat behind a huge desk covered with a mess of papers. An old, heavy adding machine with a crank teetered on the edge of the desk, and the faint smell of cigars filled the room. A Farmers Bank of Rusty Nail calendar, set to the wrong month, dangled from a nail on one of the wood-paneled walls.

"Hey there, Mozart," Wes said, looking up from his work and smiling. He wore a green eyeshade, which made him look very official. "Staying out of trouble?"

Franny nodded. "Did you go talk to Madame Malenkov

yet?" she asked nervously. "What'd she say?" All day long, she'd been worrying about the meeting. If Olga had told Wes the truth about how Franny had begged and wangled her way into the lesson deal, her parents were sure to be embarrassed and keep her from going back to "harass" the Russian.

"I haven't had time to go over there yet," Wes said. "Look at this place. The only sure things in life are death, taxes, and that your old man will always have more work than he can handle."

Franny threw herself down in one of the hard leather chairs in front of his desk, as though she was one of his customers. "Well, when *will* you have time?" she asked.

"Later," her father answered vaguely, going back to his work on one of his ledgers.

"Can I come along?" Franny nudged. She wanted to be there to manage the situation as much as possible.

"Sure."

"Can we go today? When you're finished with work? As soon as you're done?"

Wes put his pen down in amused annoyance. "All right, all right," he said, getting up. "Since you're clearly not going to let me get a moment of peace until I go over there, let's go now." He headed for the door.

Franny's heart pounded as they walked up Fair Street toward Olga's house. They climbed the porch stairs, and Wes knocked on the front door.

"Dad!" Franny hissed. "Take off your eyeshade!" Wes

was always forgetting to take it off when he left the office, sometimes wearing it to dinner or while he drank beers at Elmer's Bar. Franny knew somehow that Olga would not be terribly impressed by it.

No one answered the door, so Wes knocked again.

"Let me try," suggested Franny. She cupped her hands and called into the crack between the door and the frame: "Madame Malenkov—it's me, Franny Hansen!"

Footsteps approached the front door.

"I told you not to come until next week, *Dyevush*—" Olga said as she opened the door, stopping in midsentence when she saw Wes standing there. "Yes?" she said formally, standing up as straight as possible in her back brace.

"Hi—I'm Wes Hansen, Franny's dad," Wes said, sticking out his hand to shake Olga's. The Russian only looked at it coldly, not moving.

"Her back hurts, Dad," Franny whispered, desperately trying to put a good face on things.

Wes put his hand back down. "Oh! Sorry," he fumbled. "Well—um, welcome to Rusty Nail! The folks 'round here are real curious about meeting you."

Another stony silence followed. Franny's heart sank.

"How can I help you?" Olga said, finally.

Wes seemed taken aback. "I understand that you've offered to give Franny piano lessons," he said. "And Franny's mother and I are grateful for it. She's a real Mozart, you know."

Franny's face reddened.

"And, well, um . . . I'm sure that you're used to training some fancy students where you come from," Wes went on, twisting his eyeshade in his hands. Franny had never seen her father so nervous before! "It's just that—and I hate to say this—we can't afford to pay real steep prices. We paid her old teacher a dollar a lesson. And I just wanted to make sure that there was no misunderstanding on that count."

Olga cleared her throat. "You do not need to pay me," she said. "Your daughter and I have an arrangement. She will help me here with the housework, and if she does a good job, I *may* teach her. Nothing is for certain yet."

Franny shot the Russian a grateful look for giving her father such an edited version of their deal.

"Oh—well," said Wes. "That's really very generous of you. Are you sure that's all you need?"

"All I require is good work," Olga said. "And more importantly—absolute privacy. Good day." She began to close the door.

"I can guarantee that she won't disappoint you," Wes jabbered on. "Hey—did she tell you that I also had a chance to be a big-deal musician once—did she tell you about the time Duke Ellington came to town?"

But the door was already shut, and Olga did not open it again.

Wes just stared at it incredulously. After a few moments, they turned and walked down the stairs.

"Well, she's certainly not the . . . *warmest* person I've ever met," he said as they headed back toward Main Street. "But if this is your big chance, it's your big chance." He put his eyeshade back on and mustered up a smile for Franny. "Now let's go home and give your mother the all-clear sign."

Franny breathed a sigh of relief. "So, you really don't care about all the mean stuff that women are saying about her in the Colosseum?" she asked.

"You know what?" Wes said. "If this woman was an alien with twenty-two eyes, I'd probably still say yes if she could make you into the star you deserve to be. It's time for you to get serious."

To celebrate, he treated Franny to a huge chocolate egg-cream at the town's soda fountain—which, fortunately, ruined her appetite for the Spam supper Lorraine cooked up that evening.

The following Monday, Sandy waited for Franny outside the school.

"You're here just in time," she said excitedly. "We have five minutes before the bell. I told Runty we'd meet him at the dumpster outside the cafeteria."

"Why?" asked Franny.

Sandy looked at Franny with unrestrained impatience. "Frances," she said. "What day is it?"

"It's Monday," answered Franny.

"Correct," said Sandy. "It is Monday, October *twenty-sixth*. Do you even realize what that *means*?"

"No," said Franny.

"Have you lost your mind?" cried Sandy. "It means that we have only *five* days left until Halloween. Only five days left to plan our pranks. And guess who the prank guest of honor is this year?"

"Miss Hamm?" Franny offered.

"*No,*" Sandy thundered. "The target is Nancy Orilee, of course. And Runty says he's got a really good idea this year, involving cow poop or something."

Just then, the bell rang.

"Dang," said Sandy. "We'll have to talk to Runty after school, then. We can't do it at lunch or recess 'cause someone will overhear the plot, and it has to stay top-secret. Let's meet at the dumpster at three o'clock." She started walking toward the school.

"Sandy," Franny called, suddenly anxious. "I can't come after school. I have to be . . . somewhere."

Sandy stopped in her tracks. "What? Where?"

Franny nervously drummed her fingers on her thighs.

"So, well, I haven't had a chance to tell you, but something happened, and I have to go to Charlie's house. The spy hurt her back real bad, and if I unpack her boxes for her, she's going to give me a piano lesson. And I couldn't say no, because there's no one left in town to teach me and my parents can't afford Prancy's teacher."

"What?" shrieked Sandy. "Franny, you're a genius! Now we can *really* spy on her! Now that we'll actually be inside, I'll come along too and help. Two people always get stuff done faster than one. How'd you swing all of this?"

Franny squirmed. "When I finished painting the porch the other day, she asked me to help her," she said. "And I just forgot to tell you. But there's a small problem— I can't bring you. She said so."

"What?" said Sandy, her back stiffening. "Why?"

Franny thought quickly. "Maybe she's afraid that I'll get distracted during the lesson or something," she said.

"Fine, then I won't stay for the lesson—just the work part."

"But she said that only I should come," Franny pleaded. "But maybe if she likes me, I can talk her into letting you come too. And of course, I'll tell you *everything* I see," she added, trying to smooth things over. "And maybe she'll have some Russian candy or something that I can bring you."

A tense silence followed.

"Fine," Sandy said finally with resentment. "We'll just have to make our Halloween plans tomorrow, then, since you'll be there all afternoon today."

"Well," said Franny, cringing, "I can't do it tomorrow either. I have to help her out from Monday to Thursday, and then on Friday I get my lesson."

"You're goin' *every day?*" Sandy shouted. "Then when are we gonna plan Halloween?"

"We'll figure something out," Franny said anxiously. "Come on, we're gonna be late."

Sandy turned on her heel and marched up to the entrance. Franny scrambled after her.

"I can't believe that you sold me down the river like that," said Sandy acidly as the girls walked into the school. "Have fun with the Commie spy, since she's your new best friend."

She wouldn't even look in Franny's direction for the rest of the day.

That afternoon, Olga opened the door right away when Franny arrived.

"You will start in the music room" was her greeting. She didn't even mention Wes and Franny's visit.

Franny put down her schoolbooks in the foyer and poked her head into the music parlor. Olga and Charlie had unpacked all of her instruments and lined them up against the far wall of the room. About ten sealed boxes sat in the middle, waiting to be torn open.

"These are all filled with music scores and books," Olga informed Franny, gesturing to the box mountain stiffly. "Please take them all out and organize the books in piles alphabetically by composer. Some of the names will be written in Russian. Bring those to me, and I will tell you who the composers are."

As soon as Olga left the room, Franny sidled over to the instruments. She picked up the violin and gave it a little shake. To her disappointment, it sounded hollow. She inspected it all over to see if there were any little trapdoors in the wooden body and found none. Sandy must have been wrong about Olga smuggling nuclear parts inside.

Then she got to work. She pulled book after book out of the boxes and made neat piles along the walls. She'd never even known that so many composers had existed, and many of them had such curious, unpronounceable names like *Liszt* and *Prokofiev* and *Mussorgsky*.

In the bottom of the fourth box, she uncovered a music book written in Russian—at least, Franny *assumed* it was Russian. The title on the cover looked more like some sort of crazy code, consisting of upper- and lowercase letters, some of them even written backward:

Сергей Рахманинов

She carried it into the kitchen, where Olga sat at the table in her brace, sipping tea and reading a book written in the same kind of letters. The Russian glanced down at the score that Franny was holding and said: "That says 'Sergei Rachmaninoff.' Your favorite."

And she went right back to drinking her tea. Franny

stood there for a minute, waiting for Olga to look up again.

"Why are you still looming there?" the Russian said into her mug, not taking her eyes off the page in front of her.

"I was wondering why you have so many different instruments," Franny said. "Can you play all of them?"

"No," Olga said.

"Then why do you bring them with you everywhere?" Franny pressed.

"And why are you so nosy?" Olga countered, putting down her mug. "Do you take nosiness classes at that cowshed of a school?"

"I was just curious," Franny said. "No one else in Rusty Nail has so many. We have a piano and trumpet in my house, but no violins or anything."

Olga sighed. "My father had one of the finest rareinstrument collections in Russia. Then, when the big revolution happened there, he sent some of them to a museum in New York for safekeeping. Now I have them."

"The piano too?" asked Franny.

"No, the piano was a gift to me from the famous pianist Arthur Rubenstein."

A bit overwhelmed, Franny turned to go back to the music room. And then she stopped and asked boldly: "Madame Malenkov, if your father had so many instruments around all the time, why did you decide to play the piano instead of the viola or something?"

Olga put her cup down again in annoyance. "Because

I wanted to," she said impatiently. "Why did *you* pick the piano when there is a trumpet in your house too?"

Franny thought for a minute. " 'Cause I liked the way it sounded, I guess," she said. "I just started playing it naturally."

"That is how all musicians begin their careers," the Russian said. "They are drawn to the instrument, like a calling. Now go away."

Satisfied with what she had learned, Franny went back to her unpacking and organizing.

It took Franny the whole week to empty all of the boxes in the music room and organize the scores. She'd had to make many trips into the kitchen, since most of the books were written in Russian. By Thursday evening, her arms ached and dozens of tall piles divided the room into a complicated maze.

Olga limped into the parlor to survey the results.

"I forgot how many music books I have," she said, leaning stiffly over a pile of Haydn scores. "Okay, *Dyevushka,* I give up. Tomorrow when you come, I will give you a short lesson. Bring your old lesson books, unless they are those dreadful John Thompson ones for beginners. Leave those at home."

The next day, Franny arrived at Olga's clutching the music books that Mrs. Staudt had given her, mostly Bach.

Olga took them out of Franny's hands and examined each one.

"You will not need these again, *Dyevushka*," she said, hobbling into the kitchen. She rudely tossed them into the garbage can under the sink before Franny could even protest. "Follow me," she added as she walked back to the parlor.

Franny sat down at the piano. "No," said Olga. "That is not how we will start. Come here." The Russian stood next to the body of the piano. The piano's big lid had been propped up, and it hovered over the instrument like an enormous black wing. Franny got up and stood next to her teacher.

"Do you even know how a piano works?" Olga asked.

"I guess," said Franny. "You press a key and the sound comes out of the middle."

Olga looked most disapproving of Franny's explanation.

"In the simplest of terms, yes," she said. "Now look at this." She pointed inside the piano's belly and Franny peered in. Hundreds of parallel strings cut across the hollow space. A line of soft, fawn-colored hammers lay on top of the strings, and red felt lined the base underneath them.

"There are more than five thousand parts in the belly of this amazing creature, and it weighs over eight hundred pounds," Olga said. "Inside, there are more than two hundred strings, and each of them is stretched *very* tightly. More than 160 pounds of tension each. That means that there are eighteen *tons* of tension in this very piano. In other words, as much as six whole cars weigh. Imagine that."

Franny reached inside to pluck one of the strings. Olga smacked her hand away.

"The great composer Beethoven used to break pianos all the time," she went on. "One time, at a concert, he broke about half a dozen of those strings during the very first chords of his solo. Can you *imagine* how hard he must have been playing? What passion!"

If only Nancy Orilee had broken some strings during the Eunice Grimes visit, Franny thought. *That would've been great. But she's far too prissy to play that hard.*

"Pay attention," the Russian commanded. "Now, every time you strike a key, it is connected to a soft hammer that hits a metal string inside the piano. The sound you hear is the string vibrating. It is really much more complicated than that, but you look like you need simple explanations. This instrument is as complex and emotional as a human mind, and should always be treated with the utmost awe and respect. Now, let me see your hands again."

Franny held out her hands, and Olga lifted them up in front of Franny's face.

"Your hands are also very intricate instruments," said Olga. "Did you know that, *Dyevushka*? Each one has

nineteen bones in it, plus many joints, and dozens of ligaments and muscles that move the fingers and thumb. If
you were hanging from a cliff, your fingers could support
your whole body weight."

Franny moved her fingers and watched the bones of
her hand move. It always made her feel creepy to imagine
her skeleton under her skin.

"It is very important that you learn these things,"
Olga said. "Loving music is not enough to play it, and just
wanting to be the best will not make you the best. You
must understand your body and the instrument very well.
Otherwise, both your knowledge and your music will be
superficial. Now, there is your first lesson."

"That's all?" cried Franny.

Olga nodded. But she limped over to one of the book
piles and picked up a Beethoven score.

"Take this home with you and start learning the two
pieces," she said. "If you do a good job with your chores
next week, you may play for me and I will instruct you."

Franny didn't dare protest, but she scowled. All of that
work and heavy lifting and organizing for a lousy ten-
minute lesson! If this was the best that Olga had to offer,
maybe she should ask Mrs. Staudt to take her back.

Olga watched her. "I know what you are thinking,"
she said with a little smile. "From that sour look on your
face. I do not teach pieces from scratch. You must go
home and learn the music first, and then we will have
something to work with next week."

"Does this mean that you'll give me a *real* lesson next Friday?" Franny asked sullenly.

"That depends," said Olga. "You know the terms of our deal. Now, I have a list of groceries that I need before you go home for the night."

Franny trudged over to Hans Zimmerman's store, squinting in the late-afternoon sunlight and clutching a few dollar bills in her hand. Maybe Sandy had been right—everyone in this town seemed to think that she was a free hired hand. If Sandy had known what was going on inside Olga's house, she'd have laughed for hours and said: "Boy, did you get duped, Franny."

Chapter Twelve

Franny woke up that Saturday morning with the uncomfortable feeling that she'd forgotten something. She lay in her bed, staring at the ceiling and trying to remember what it was. Suddenly she sat up with a jolt.

It was Halloween!

Tonight at six o'clock, the school would host its big annual costume parade in the gym, and after that, everyone would run off to go trick-or-treating. Franny kicked off the sheets and covers and ran into the kitchen, where Lorraine was drinking coffee with Mrs. Charity Engebraten.

"Mom!" Franny exclaimed. "We completely forgot about Halloween! Do we still have my ghost costume from last year?"

A sheepish look crossed Lorraine's face. "Oops—I think I shredded that old sheet to use as cleaning rags," she said. "But I'll see if there's something else you can use." She left the room and padded down the hall to the linen closet. Mrs. Engebraten slurped her coffee and looked Franny up and down.

"So," the woman said. "I hear you're startin' piano lessons with Charlie Koenig's uppity Commie wife."

Franny just nodded and walked over to the refrigerator. She couldn't stand Mrs. Engebraten.

"I wonder if that woman is ever goin' to come out of that house," Mrs. Engebraten continued, talking more to herself than to Franny. "Guess she thinks she's too good to mix with the common folks of Rusty Nail. Either that, or she's hidin' out over there, puttin' together an atomic bomb to put under our church."

Franny reached for the milk. "For your information, she hurt her back and that's why she's staying inside," she said. "And anyway, you should mind your own business."

Mrs. Engebraten gasped. "Well, I never," she said. "If I was your mother, I'd wash your mouth out with a big bar of soap."

"It's a good thing you're not my mother, then," retorted Franny.

Mrs. Engebraten narrowed her eyes. "I'd watch out if I was you, Little Miss Big Mouth," she said. " 'Cause people 'round town are gonna start gettin' the wrong idea about you if you keep hangin' around that woman."

Just then, Lorraine walked back into the kitchen. "This is all I could find, honey," she said apologetically. She shook out an old sheet covered with pictures of robots and space-ships.

"Mo-o-om!" Franny wailed in chagrin. "I can't wear that! Why couldn't you have cut up this sheet instead of my ghost costume?"

"Of course you can wear it," Lorraine said, fishing the scissors out of the kitchen junk drawer. "It even has a nice futuristic theme for Halloween." She snipped out two jagged eyeholes in the middle and handed it to Franny. "There you go, sweetheart."

Franny snatched it out of her mother's hands and stomped down the hallway to her room. As she went, she heard Mrs. Engebraten say to Lorraine: "That one's get-tin' a little big for her britches, isn't she?"

Franny slammed her bedroom door and glowered at the ghost costume. Nancy Orilee was going to laugh her head off. Already thinking of revenge, Franny couldn't wait to see Sandy before the parade and hear what plans she and Runty had cooked up for their annual Halloween prank.

Sandy had given Franny the cold shoulder all week. But since Halloween only came once a year, she agreed to meet Franny before the school parade.

Both Sandy and Runty wore vampire costumes with

black capes and big, sharp fake teeth, another purchase from the Finkelstein Prank & Curiosity Company. They stood together outside the entrance to the gym when Franny arrived.

"Hey, guys," Franny called out uneasily as she approached them. She carried the hated robot sheet under her arm, waiting until the last possible moment to put it on. Then she sniffed the air. "Why do you both smell like hot dogs?" she asked.

"Iths th' kethip," said Sandy around her fake fangs. "Wer uthing it ath fak brud."

"What?" said Franny.

Sandy spit out her fangs and said: "It's the ketchup. We're using it as fake blood." She produced a red plastic squeeze bottle of ketchup from under her cape.

"Gimmeshum," said Runty from behind his fangs, and gingerly applied some to his chin.

"So what's the Nancy plan?" Franny asked in a hushed voice.

"Wel-l-l," said Sandy, eyeing Franny as sternly as a judge. "I don't even know that we should tell you, since you didn't bother to help us plan it."

"Yeah," said Runty.

"Oh, come on, guys," Franny pleaded. "You know I wanted to help. Tell me what you're gonna do."

Sandy could never resist the urge to flaunt her own genius. "We wanted to do something with cow dung— you know, make some sort of booby trap where she'd slip and fall down into it," she said confidentially. "But it got real complicated. So, in the end, we had to come up with somethin' else."

"Yeah," said Runty. Grinning, he pointed at the ketchup bottle. Franny's heart pounded.

"Are you going to squirt that on Nancy Orilee's costume? Right now, in front of all these people?" she asked.

"Yep," said Sandy. "Accidentally, of *course*."

As if on cue, Nancy Orilee and her mother pranced past them toward the gym entrance. In a deliciously cruel twist of fate, Nancy wore a snow white leotard with a tutu and a set of fairy wings made of pale feathers. She looked at Sandy and Runty with disgust.

"I see that your parents can't afford to take you to the dentist, Sandy Anne," she said, taking delicate little steps into the gym. "Can't *wait* to see your costume this year, Frances." She didn't even bother to address Runty, who stood there doltishly drooling around his fake teeth.

"Oh Lordy, lemme at her," said Sandy, clutching at the ketchup bottle.

"Are you *really* going to pour that on her?" Franny asked nervously. "It'll completely ruin her costume." Franny certainly despised Nancy Orilee as much as anyone—more so, probably—but the idea of sousing her with ketchup in front of a gaggle of teachers and parents seemed outright foolhardy.

"Yes, we are, and yes, it will," said Sandy testily. "You're like an old lady tonight, Franny, makin' me repeat everything I say. Here, I brought three bottles. Take one and hide it under your costume. Hey—where *is* your costume?"

Franny shook out the sheet. Sandy moaned when she saw it, and Runty guffawed, spraying them with spittle. Franny sighed and pulled the sheet over her head, tugging it this way and that until the holes were over her eyes. Struggling not to trip, she followed Sandy and Runty into the gym.

The room was packed with teachers, parents, and dozens of kids in costumes: little witches, scarecrows, and, of course, farmers. Sandy, Runty, and Franny took their places with the other fifth graders and waited for their turn to parade around the gym. Franny could hear people snickering at her sheet.

"This is what we'll do," whispered Sandy. "I'll make sure that we're in line right behind her. When we're walking around, I'll pretend to trip on Franny's hem, and, Runty—you pretend to trip over me. Then we'll send the ketchup flying! Got it?"

"I don't know if we should do this," Franny said uneasily. "We're going to get in a whole lot of trouble."

Sandy's face grew red. "Look here, Franny," she fumed. "We're doing this for *you*. After all, Prancy is *your* number one enemy. Now—*are you in or are you out?*"

Franny looked at Nancy Orilee prancing around at the head of the line, saying over and over again: "I'm the beautiful sugarplum fairy! The star of *The Nutcracker*!"

and then, to an admiring first grader: "Don't touch my wings, or else." It *would* serve her right to be embarrassed in front of all these people, Franny reasoned.

But then she saw her parents come into the gym and wave at her. Franny's heart sank. Wes would be so disappointed in her if she got in trouble again. Who knew—he might even get mad enough to ground her from going to Olga's house, and the Russian would *never* take her back if Franny abruptly stopped coming. Their deal already seemed tenuous enough. When she thought about it this way, Franny made up her mind. She turned back to Sandy.

"You guys do it," Franny said. "I can't."

Sandy glared at her and Franny's knees went weak. She opened her mouth to apologize—but before she could, Sandy reached out and snatched the bottle away from Franny. Then she grabbed Runty by the elbow, and the two of them marched up to the front of the line and stood right behind Nancy.

Then Mr. Moody called out over the crowd: "Miss Hamm! Get your troops in order!"

At that moment, the school band started playing a marching song. Amidst the blatting trombones and crashing cymbals, all of the parents and kids in the gym clapped. Even Mayor Reverend Jerry was there, standing next to Mr. Moody and waiting to give out a prize for the best costume.

The fifth-grade mob lurched forward, marching in time to the music. Gretchen Beasley, appropriately dressed as a baby, shuffled along in front of Franny. It took all of Franny's concentration just to keep the cut-out eyeholes in the right place. She had only gone about twenty feet when someone let out a bloodcurdling scream on the other side of the gym.

"My costume!" shrieked Nancy Orilee. "Sandy and Runty *ruined* my beautiful costume!"

She burst into angry sobs. Franny yanked the sheet over her head and saw Miss Hamm, Mr. Moody, and Mrs. Orilee running to the aid of the victim. A pulpy stream of ketchup dripped from her wings and leotard onto the floor. All of the kids in the gym shrieked with laughter. "Serves ya right!" yelled Harold Hrapp before his mother stepped in and shushed him.

"It was an accident!" shouted Sandy. "I tripped on my cape and Runty fell right over me, and then the ketchup just went flyin' everywhere!"

Utterly unconvinced, Mr. Moody clapped his hand down on Sandy's shoulder and pushed her toward the gym exit. "Get over here, Mr. Knutson," he said to Runty.

Runty grunted and spat out his fangs. "Aw, *man*," he said as he galumphed out of the gym.

A fleet of mothers gathered around Nancy, wiping her off and cooing. Mayor Reverend Jerry shouted: "Keep on movin', fifth graders! 'Round the gym you go!" And all of the parents clapped and cheered. Franny put her sheet back on and scurried forward.

After every grade had trucked around in a big circle, the

kids ran outside to start their trick-or-treating. However, since Franny's regular Halloween partner had been imprisoned in Mr. Moody's office, she had no one to go with. She stood awkwardly with her parents at the gym exit.

Lorraine was horrified by Sandy's prank.

"I just don't understand what gets into that girl sometimes," she said. "She gets wilder all the time."

"Maybe she feels outshone or something," Wes said, and looked down at Franny. "Looks to me like she wants attention."

"What do you mean?" asked Franny.

"Well, you've been getting a lot of attention yourself lately," said Wes. "With your big concert and everything. Maybe Sandy Anne feels jealous that you stand out so much and she doesn't—so she's acting out."

This didn't make a lot of sense to Franny. "But she doesn't even play the piano," she objected. "She told me herself that all she wants is to be a regular girl and fool around and stuff."

"People are funny that way," Wes said. "They say one thing and feel another, sometimes without even knowing it. I'm proud of you for staying out of trouble tonight," he added. "I'm willing to bet that you were real tempted to throw a little ketchup on Nancy yourself, Mozart."

Franny looked away, embarrassed. The three of them walked home past all of the brightly lit houses of Rusty Nail. Kids ran from front door to front door, tugging paper bags and pails of candy loot along with them. Franny wished she could join in as well, but the prospect of trick-or-treating alone—or worse, escorted by her parents—was too mortifying.

They walked past Charlie and Olga's house. The lights downstairs had all been turned off, and the house seemed vacant. Franny noticed that the Russian had thoughtfully left a basket of apples on the front porch for trick-or-treaters. But every time kids reached her lawn, their parents abruptly steered them away.

When Franny walked past the house again the next morning, the basket still sat there, its contents untouched. To her shock, she saw that someone had scrawled, in red chalk, on the sidewalk in front of the house:

Commie–Go home!

Fortunately, however, it rained that morning, and the ugly words were washed away by lunchtime.

For the next week, Franny kept a grueling schedule that went roughly like this:

7 a.m.: Get up and get ready for school
8 a.m.–2:45 p.m.: School
3 p.m.–5:30 p.m.: Work at Olga's house

6 p.m.–7 p.m.: Dinner at home
7 p.m.–8 p.m.: Homework
8 p.m.–9:30 p.m.: Practice piano

On Friday morning, Lorraine had to wake Franny up three times before the girl got out of bed. Franny sleepily ate a bowl of Lorraine's gravelly oatmeal as her mother watched her with concern.

"How much longer are you going to work for Mrs. Koenig after school?" Lorraine asked. All week, Franny had been shelving Olga's music books and unpacking the other boxes.

"She doesn't like to be called 'Mrs. Koenig,'" said Franny.

"What?" said Lorraine. "What does she like to be called, then?"

Franny blearily shoved another spoonful of soggy cereal into her mouth. "Madame Malenkov," she reported.

"Oh," said Lorraine. "That's right. How long did she and your dad agree that you'd work for her?"

"We didn't say," Franny said dully. "As long as I'm a good helper, she'll give me a lesson at the end of every week."

"Oh," said Lorraine again. "What are you working on in the lessons?"

"She taught me how a piano works, and about my

hands," Franny said. "And she threw away my Bach books. She hates Bach, so we're learning Beethoven this week."

"She threw away your books?" exclaimed Lorraine. "How presumptuous! Maybe we should ask Mrs. Staudt to take you back."

"I don't want to go back to Mrs. Staudt!" cried Franny. "Then I'll be right back where I started." Even as she said this, she thought about her skimpy first lesson with Olga and wondered how much progress she was actually making.

"Hmph," said Lorraine, unconvinced. "Well, at the very least, I think you should tell her that you need to come home earlier each day. I don't think it's healthy for a girl your age to work so hard."

"Hard work never hurt anyone," grumbled Wes as he staggered into the kitchen, his hair sticking up everywhere. He was always terribly crabby in the morning.

"I'll tell her, okay?" Franny promised, feeling guilty since she had no intention of telling the Russian any such thing.

Lorraine looked out the window. "I just hope these lessons are worth all of this trouble in the end," she said, more to herself than anyone else.

"Of course they will be," said Wes, fumbling with the coffeepot.

Lorraine looked down at Franny. Picking up her daughter's hand, she squeezed each slender finger protectively.

"I hope so, sweetheart," she said after a minute, and kissed Franny's forehead.

And thus reassured, Franny collected her backpack and music book and walked to school.

Franny went to Olga's that afternoon after school, as usual. The Russian opened the door right away.

"Come in, come in," she said. "I have much for you to do today." Although her back was still tender, she had stopped wearing her brace a few days earlier, and her movements were much more graceful.

Franny walked into the foyer. "Madame Malenkov, it's Friday," she said. "Aren't I supposed to get my lesson today? I worked all week on opening the boxes and stuff, and I've been practicing the Beethoven real hard."

"You mean 'I've been practicing *very* hard,' " Olga corrected her, walking into the parlor. "Try not to sound like a peasant, *Dyevushka*."

"You know what I mean," said Franny. "So do I get my lesson?"

"All right—I give up," said Olga, throwing up her hands in mock surrender. "I will listen to your Beethoven, such as it is."

Franny ran into the parlor room, practically threw herself onto the piano bench, and propped her music book up in front of her. Olga nodded, and Franny began playing the pieces she'd been practicing all week.

Instead of falling asleep like Mrs. Staudt, Olga stood over Franny and watched her every move, giving rapid-fire commands: "Stop! Do that phrase again! Bring your thumb under your hand like so, and yes! Much better fingering!" "This says *forte,* so play it louder!" "Now it is *staccato*—so pluck the keys! The sound must be crisp and fast—like a machine gun! Rat-tat-tat-tat-tat!" "And now it's *legato*—yes, very good! It must be smooth, like a stream of water!" And so on and so forth.

As Franny scrambled to keep up, she thought about her first lesson and imagined the ligaments and muscles in her hands working hard and getting stronger, and the hammers striking the tensed strings inside the belly of the mighty piano. She could hardly believe that so much effort and machinery went into producing the ephemeral notes that shimmered in the air—and then disappeared forever.

By the time they finished the lesson, exhaustion filled her arms. She looked at a clock on the shelves and realized with shock that the lesson had lasted nearly an hour! She could hardly believe that Olga had given her so much time. Clearly, she was rising in her teacher's estimation.

Olga picked out another music book from her collection and leafed through it to select Franny's next piece.

"This is the one I want you to learn for next week," she said, handing the score over to Franny. "And practice the Beethoven some more too. And so you know: Charles is coming back tomorrow, but I would still like you to come. In other words, I am prepared to extend our arrangement."

Franny's face flushed with pride. "Okay," she said almost shyly.

"Now can you please clean up the kitchen for me before you go?" Olga asked. "I'm going to lie down upstairs. My back feels like it has pins and needles in it."

Franny ran down the hallway, filled with the satisfaction that comes with getting a good grade or an award. Things were *finally* going her way. She washed dishes and dried them, humming bits of the Beethoven piece they'd just practiced and daydreaming about playing it in front of a big audience. When the phone on the wall rang, she picked it up automatically.

"Hello?"

There was a long pause, and then a deep voice on the other end said: "Charles Koenig, please."

"He's not here," said Franny, putting a dish into the cupboard.

"Can you tell me if there is an Olga Malenkov there?" the man asked.

"Sure, I'll get her," Franny said, and then her heart froze. Olga had told her to never, *ever* answer the phone, and in her reverie, Franny had completely forgotten her instructions.

Her hands trembled as she tried to figure out what to do. Fetching Olga, or even telling her that she'd broken one of the cardinal rules, would clearly mean the end of the lessons. With a sense of dread, Franny realized that her only option was to tell another lie. She cupped her hand over the receiver for a minute, and then worked up her courage to talk again.

"I was wrong; she's not here either," whispered Franny, praying that Olga hadn't heard the phone ring.

"Is that so," said the man.

"Yes," managed Franny, her voice wavering. "She went out."

"Well, tell her that we'll be in touch," the caller said.

"Who is this?" asked Franny.

But the man hung up without another word.

Not a sound came from upstairs. Olga must have fallen asleep. Thanking her lucky stars, Franny quickly put the dishes away and ran all the way home.

Chapter Thirteen

On a Sunday afternoon several weeks later, Franny lay on the living-room couch listening to the radio when a loud crash came from the kitchen. She scurried in and found Lorraine kneeling over an enormous blob of mashed potatoes filled with ceramic shards from the broken casserole dish.

"Ohhh," wailed Lorraine. "I don't have time to run out and get more potatoes, and Aunt Lillian and Uncle Gustave are coming over for supper. Franny, if I give you some money, can you run down to the store for me?"

Franny ambled down to old Hans Zimmerman's grocery store, where she promptly wasted a good chunk of time loitering around the meager newspaper and candy section. She pulled a few dusty copies of *Life* magazine from earlier that year out from the creaky magazine rack. Hans ordered in shipments of glossy magazines every month, but sometimes they turned up and sometimes they didn't. This was just as well, for most of the folks around town didn't read high-end literature like *Life*. *The Old Farmer's Almanack* was usually as fancy as it got.

Franny lazily leafed through a few of the magazines. In the middle of the third one, she saw an article titled:

RUSSIA AFTER STALIN

Ignoring the text, Franny instead looked at the pictures of buildings with roofs shaped like huge onions, soldier parades, and a man with a big mustache lying on a tomb. She was about to stuff the magazine back in the rack when a headline caught her attention:

GENIUS, GLORY, AND TRAGEDY:
THE SAGA OF PIANIST OLGA MALENKOV

Franny almost dropped the magazine from surprise. She could hardly believe that Olga, Rusty Nail's very own resident Commie, was splashed across the pages of an important magazine! A couple of pictures of her teacher accompanied the article. The first one showed the Russian dressed in a lavish gown, standing on a stage bowing to an audience of hundreds. The second was a disturbing, official-looking head shot in which Olga gave a penetrating stare into the camera.

Franny sat down behind one of the fruit stands, where Hans wouldn't see her, and scoured the article. At first, the magazine talked about what a great pianist Olga was (nothing she hadn't heard over and over again from Olga herself)—and then it got interesting:

> Miss Malenkov was born an only child to an aristocratic family in 1924, the same year Lenin died and Stalin rose to power. As anti-Communists and loyalists to the czar, her parents, Hertzog (Duke) Alexander Malenkov and his wife, Sofia, had been in hiding in the Russian countryside for five years. When Stalin began his infamous purges of his enemies in 1937, the duke and duchess sent the thirteen-year-old girl on a daring escape out of the country, carrying forged travel documents and money sealed in a violin.

So Sandy had been right about Olga smuggling things around in her violin! The article continued:

Following her terrifying journey, which took her through Romania, Bulgaria, and Turkey, Miss Malenkov boarded a series of ships that ultimately took her to New York City. There she was taken in by distant relatives who had defected from Russia in 1917. A talented pianist, she entered the prestigious Juilliard School and began performing publicly at the age of fourteen. She never saw her parents again.

Just then, before Franny could read any further, the bell on the front door tinkled and a couple of pairs of heels clicked officiously in.

"Hi there, Hans—d'you mind if we hang one of these flyers up in your window?"

It was just that busybody Norma Smitty. Still keeping a low profile, Franny peered around the corner of the shelves to see what the woman was up to. Melba stood next to her with a sheath of handwritten notices in her arms.

"What is it?" asked Hans, creakily leaning forward to examine the notices.

"Oh, nothin' really," said Melba. "It's just about a new club that we're formin' for the ladies in town. It's called the W-O-R-N-A-T-C-T."

"That's a real long name," said Hans, impressed. "What's it stand fer?"

"Women of Rusty Nail Against the Commie Threat," Norma announced proudly. "Or the Communist Threat, if you wanna be formal about things. Anyway, we're gonna have a meetin' every Sunday in the back room of the church. We all have to do our part, you know."

Suddenly the bell tinkled again. When Hans saw the incoming customer, he was so surprised that his top dentures fell out onto the counter with a plasticky clatter. As Franny craned her neck to see who it was, she heard a familiar voice say: "Good afternoon. I would like a bottle of milk, some coffee, and some sugar, please."

It was Olga! Franny's heart nearly stopped and fell into her stomach. What on earth was *she* doing here? She *never* came shopping—usually Charlie or Franny did it for her. In a hurry, Franny stuffed the *Life* magazine under some potatoes, not wanting to be seen with it. Olga was extremely protective of her privacy, and there Franny sat, plain as day, reading about the deepest, darkest moments of the Russian's past.

Hans fumbled on the counter for his teeth and jammed them back into his mouth.

"We're all outta coffee," he said. "But we got sugar and milk right there in the back of the store. Help yerself."

Norma and Melba glared at Olga with as much ice and venom as they could muster. The Russian ignored their rude stares as she walked to the back of the store to get a bag of sugar.

"Well, look at that," Melba said in a loud whisper. "She's wearin' silk stockings to do the grocery shoppin', but she can't be bothered to wear them to church."

"And look at that fur coat," Norma rasped. "Who's she tryin' to impress? It's like she's lettin' everyone know that the Queen's arrived at last."

Olga walked back to the front of the room. As she passed Melba and Norma, she nodded coolly to both of them. Then she paid old Hans for the milk and sugar and opened the front door.

"Wait a minute, Mrs. Koenig," Norma called. Olga stopped, the blustery breeze outside fluttering the collar on her fur coat. "Please take one of our flyers. I think you might really enjoy our new club."

"Thank you," Olga said, taking the folded piece of paper. When she opened and read it, a peculiar, crooked smile crossed her face. She folded it up again, dropped it into her grocery bag, and looked up at Norma and Melba.

"A club in my honor—how flattering," she said with deadpan dignity. "I will certainly try to come by." And she left, the door clanging shut behind her.

"Lordy, that was gutsy of you, Norma," giggled Melba.

Norma looked prouder than a newly inaugurated president. "Just lettin' her know what's what," she said. "It's only fair to let yer enemy know that the battle's about to start. Come on, we still got the rest of Main Street to paper before we call it a day." And they sailed out of the store.

Franny sat back on the floor with a thud. She knew that all of the women from the Colosseum hated the *idea* of Olga, but usually all they did was talk meanly about people behind their backs, not confront them directly. And what did Norma mean by *battle*? They weren't going to try to hurt Olga, were they? She was so disturbed that she ran home empty-handed.

Lorraine met her at the front door.

"Where on earth have you *been*?" she cried. *"And where are the potatoes?"*

"I forgot them," Franny said, her face reddening, and she told her mother everything that had happened at the grocery store—from the magazine to the newly launched charter of W.O.R.N.A.T.C.T.

"Well, I swear," Lorraine said, her wooden spoon dripping lumpy gravy on the floor. "I can't believe those silly women sometimes."

"Why can't they just leave Madame Malenkov alone?" exclaimed Franny. "She never even bothers anyone, but all they can talk about is how having a Commie in town is like having a plague here. I see Madame Malenkov all the time, and she never talks about hating America or blowing us up or anything."

Lorraine shoved a turkey into the oven. "I'm sure that Norma and Melba think that they're doing a good thing," she said, standing up and wiping her hands on a dishrag. "Everyone sees things differently. When you look at Mrs. Koenig—I mean, Madame Malenkov—you see a very private woman who is giving you an opportunity that you wouldn't have had otherwise."

Franny blushed as her mother went on.

"But all they see is a mysterious Russian woman who seemed to come out of nowhere, and in their minds, that spells trouble. Politicians have been telling us bad things about the Commies for so long that some people get scared and do foolish things, like form this club."

"You're not going to make me stop taking lessons with Madame Malenkov now that all of your friends hate her so much, are you?" pressed Franny.

Lorraine sighed. "Of course not," she said. "But it's not as easy a decision as I'd like it to be. Your father is right; you need this opportunity. But I wish . . . there weren't these problems with Madame Malenkov. After all, we have to live here in Rusty Nail—not just you, but me and Daddy and Owen and Jessie. And it's hard thinking that people might look at us funny for letting you spend so much time with the Russian lady."

"So why are you letting me take lessons at all?" Franny asked, feeling a little bit guilty for putting her family in this position.

"I guess because I trust Charlie," Lorraine said. "And

your father wants big things to happen for you so badly. So I tell myself—what would a dangerous Commie want with Rusty Nail? People in this town just want more drama and excitement in their lives, and this is Norma's way of convincing herself that Rusty Nail is more important than it really is.

"Besides, that silly club will be like a rocking chair to Norma and the other ladies," she continued. "It'll give them something to do, and get them nowhere. They'll just stand around the Colosseum on Sundays, gabbing as usual."

Franny giggled. "I'm telling Dad that you said 'Colosseum,'" she said.

"I *did*?" Lorraine exclaimed. "Well, I didn't mean it. Now go down to the store and get me some more potatoes this instant."

As Franny ran down the front stairs, her mother called after her: "And bring back that old copy of *Life* as well!"

"I have a treat for you, *Dyevushka*," Olga said as she opened the front door for Franny the next day. "Follow me." She walked into the music room and put a record on the player.

"Listen to this," she said excitedly. "It just arrived in a package from New York." She put the needle on the record, and a wonderful piano concerto played from the speakers. When it was over, Olga turned to her and said: "Well? What did you think?"

"I loved it," said Franny, wondering why Olga was beaming. "What was it?"

"Rachmaninoff, of course!" Olga exclaimed. "Who else? And guess who was playing it? *Me!*"

"That was *you* on the record?" shouted Franny, running over to look at the label. Sure enough, it proclaimed:

Sergei Rachmaninoff, Piano Concerto no. 2 in C Minor Played by Olga Malenkov and the New York Philharmonic

"We recorded it last year, but this is the first time I have heard it," Olga said.

"I can't believe it," said Franny, flabbergasted. "I have a question, though: why do you like Rachmaninoff so much?"

"Because his music is like Russia itself," Olga said grandly. "Romantic, tumultuous, and treacherous. It is my life's tragedy that I will probably never go back."

"Why can't you?" pressed Franny.

"For lots of reasons," said Olga, looking somber. "That is enough talking now—you have work to do."

Franny began unpacking boxes of Olga's regular books in the living room. Her stomach still jumped when she thought about the article in the grocery store, and Olga's comment about never going back to Russia only made her feel more tense. Finally, when she took a Russian book into the kitchen for Olga to identify, she decided to bring it up.

"Madame Malenkov? I, uh . . . I was in the grocery store yesterday while you were there."

"Yes," said Olga. "I saw you there, hidden away in the corner."

Franny's face reddened. "Oh," she said. "Well, I just wanted to say that I hated the way that Norma and Melba acted in there."

"Yes, well, I guess that they do not know any better," Olga said, looking into her teacup. "They even sent me a little present afterward."

She picked up a folded letter from the kitchen table and handed it to Franny, who gasped when she read it:

> Notice from the W.O.R.N.A.T.C.T.
> The Women of Rusty Nail
> are watching you!
>   All suspicious activity
> will be reported to the
> authorities. We're serious!
> So you better watch out!

Olga took the note back and reread the missive. "They did not even have the courage to sign it."

"Sometimes I hate Rusty Nail," Franny blurted out.

"Most folks around here think that they're so all-American and Christian and welcoming, but then they turn around and start mean clubs and stuff like that."

"That is called hypocrisy," said Olga. "And it is everywhere, not just Rusty Nail. I would not get too upset about it if I were you."

"That's easy for you to say," said Franny. "You're a famous pianist and can leave anytime you want. I bet you hate it here and can't wait to get away."

"I do not hate Rusty Nail as much as you think," Olga said. "I have very specific reasons for being here, and I am not ready to leave just yet. And anyway, it could be worse. In most American small towns, people use only words as weapons against you. What is that saying you have here, the one about the sticks?"

"Sticks and stones may break my bones, but names can never hurt me," Franny recited automatically.

"Yes, that's it. Here it is mostly name-calling, but where I come from, they use more than just sticks and stones. They use blades and bullets against entire families."

"What do you mean?" Franny asked.

"Haven't you ever heard of Stalin?" Olga asked irritably. "What *are* they teaching you in that school—how to grow corn?"

Franny frowned. "I know who he is," she said. "He was the evil Communist leader of Russia, the one who just died. But why would he kill Russians? I thought he only wanted to kill Americans with nuclear bombs and stuff."

Olga looked at the wall. "I really do not want to talk about this anymore," she said. "You have a lot to learn, and I do not want to be the one to teach you about it."

Franny remembered the part of the article about the "purges" and how Olga never saw her parents again.

"Madame Malenkov," she asked, "did Stalin want to kill *your* family?"

"Must I spell it out for you, *Dyevushka?*" Olga asked. "My parents are dead. They were Russian but they were not Communists. They were murdered for their political views, and I am the only one left. So, believe me—I am no Commie either. And that is all you need to know. Now please go finish the books."

Franny walked back to the living room in shock. She didn't dare go back into the kitchen for the rest of the afternoon.

Chapter Fourteen

Ever since Halloween, Franny simply had not been able
to get Sandy to talk to her. Once Sandy's suspension from
school was over and she came back to the classroom,
Franny tried all sorts of tricks to get her friend's attention.
She tried passing Sandy notes during class, but every time
Sandy stalked up to the trash bin in the front of the room
and threw them away unread. If Franny tried to sit near
her in the lunchroom, Sandy would snatch up her lunch
tray and go sit at another table.

The last straw was this: one day, before class, Franny
brought in a box of Red Hots and left it with a note inside
Sandy's desk. Sandy trotted in and, as usual, sat down
without looking in Franny's direction. When she opened

up the desk and saw the candy, she took out the box and eyed the note. And then she said: "Hey, Runty, c'mere. I got somethin' for you."

Runty dutifully clomped over and ripped the top off the cardboard box. He poured every single Red Hot into his mouth and threw the box on the floor. As he trudged back to his desk, he gave Franny a toothy grin, a few of the sticky candy pieces falling out of his mouth.

Franny's face burned. Sandy was playing hardball. Franny resolved to find her after school and hash things out once and for all.

That afternoon, when the bell rang and everyone ran out of the classroom, Franny collected her things and walked toward their usual haunts on Main Street. She marched up to Hans Zimmerman's general store and pushed open the front door.

To her disappointment, only old Hans and Mayor Reverend Jerry were there. They sat together at the front counter while old Hans idly slapped at a lazy fly with a rolled-up newspaper.

"Dang, Hans," said Mayor Reverend Jerry. "Why don't you just get some fly spray and put that thing out of its misery? Every time I come in here, you're sittin' here, swattin' at that fly."

"Nah, I couldn't do that," old Hans said slowly, gnawing away on a piece of tough old beef jerky.

"Why not?" asked the mayor.

"Well," said Hans. "It's just that the fly's been around here for so long. It's kinda like an old friend. I'd be real lonely without it."

"My Lord, you're a fool if I've ever seen one," Mayor Reverend Jerry said amicably. "Are you sure you should be eatin' this stuff with your wobbly ole fake teeth?" And then: "Oh, hi there, Franny Hansen. What're you doin' sneakin' around over there by the candy?"

"Have you seen Sandy?" Franny asked.

"Nah," said old Hans. "Her parents called me and tole me not to sell her any candy, so she don't come in here no more."

Disappointed, Franny walked toward the front door. Where could Sandy be?

"Jest a minute, Franny," said Mayor Reverend Jerry, reaching for a piece of jerky. "Word 'round town is that you're takin' pian-er lessons with Charlie Koenig's new wife. Madame Badame, or whatever she calls herself."

Franny scowled. She'd heard enough banter about Olga in this store to last a good long while. "So what if I am," she said.

"Hmm," said the mayor, as though pondering a fascinating fact. "D'you ever see anything out of the ordinary in the house?"

"No," lied Franny, automatically thinking of the mysterious phone call.

"It is kinda strange," drawled the mayor. "We've all

been waitin' to meet her, and she never even comes to hear my preachin', or even to say hello. I'm downright insulted. And then I get to wonderin'—why would a lady from Russia want to come to Rusty Nail in the first place? I'm worried that she might be tryin' to spread Commie propaganda, and that she's startin' with our young folks."

"She's not a Commie spy," Franny snapped. "She's not even a Commie, for your information!"

She ran out of the store, the front door slapping shut behind her.

But then another "out of the ordinary" event *did* take place, several days after Franny's exchange with Mayor Reverend Jerry and old Hans.

Franny had just left Olga's for the evening. Charlie was out of town again for another trial. The black night sky hung heavily over the town, and Franny's breath froze in powdery tufts in the cold air. Warm yellow light edged out from behind the closed curtains of the houses as families sat down for supper or listened to their favorite evening radio shows.

All of a sudden a strange car rounded the corner and drove up the street toward the Oak and Fair streets crossroads. Franny stopped and stared at it. In a town as small as Rusty Nail, where people could even tell the difference between a Hellickson pig and a Klompenhower one, everyone knew their neighbors' cars and trucks. This dark sedan might as well have come from a different planet.

Franny just *knew* that it must be heading to Olga's. Her heart pounding, she followed the car back up to the crossroads, running through backyards so that the car's driver wouldn't see her.

Sure enough, the car silently pulled up in front of the Koenig-Malenkov residence and parked at the curb. From Thelma Britches' yard, Franny watched as two strangers wearing overcoats and fedora hats got out and marched up the path. She snuck around the side of Olga's house to her old station behind the peony bush, which had a good view of the front porch.

The men walked up the front stairs, and one of them reached out and rang the doorbell. Franny heard Olga calling: "*Dyevushka?* What did you forget this time?" Her footsteps approached the front door, and suddenly the light from inside poured out over the men on the porch.

"Olga Malenkov?" one of them asked gruffly. The other just stared at the Russian with hostility.

Franny's stomach clenched in apprehension. What if they were the same people who had killed Olga's parents back in Russia? Should she shout for help? But even if she did—who in Rusty Nail would come to the aid of the Commie?

"Who wants to know?" Olga demanded boldly.

One of the men reached into the breast pocket of his coat. Franny almost fainted, thinking that he was going to pull out a gun. Instead, he produced a sealed envelope and handed it to Olga.

"You can run, but you can't hide," he said. "Consider yourself served. This is an official summons, and I'd show up if I were you."

And with that, the two men stomped back down the porch stairs, got into their car, and drove away into the darkness. Olga slammed her front door shut.

Franny fell back against the house and took a couple of deep breaths. Who *were* those men? Were they related to that strange phone call? And what did they mean by *summons*? The word conjured up an image of a genie in Franny's mind, which made no sense.

She wished that she could talk to someone about what she'd seen—but telling her parents was out of the question, and Sandy clearly wanted nothing to do with her.

Franny didn't see anyone else on the streets as she walked home, and she hoped that no one had glimpsed the strange car from their windows. Olga already had enough problems with the townspeople of Rusty Nail.

Chapter Fifteen

The next day was Saturday. After breakfast, Franny set up her music on the piano and began to practice. Wes ambled out of the kitchen and stood next to the piano, plate in hand. He was eating pie for breakfast since he said that Lorraine's rubbery fried eggs were "too much to face before the coffee kicks in."

"You know, Mozart," he said, polishing off the last of the crust. "Your mother might be right. Maybe you're working too hard. How 'bout a break?"

"I thought you said that hard work never hurt anyone," Franny said, turning a page.

"Well, if we're going to make a *real* musician out of you, we're going to have to teach you about Work-Hard-Play-Hard," her father answered. "Do you know what that is?"

Franny shook her head. "Some sort of game?" she guessed.

Wes smiled. "It's a way of life," he said. "It means that if you work hard, you should also get to play hard—especially a big-shot musician like you. Let's go down to Hauser's after lunch and catch a matinee."

A few hours later, they walked down Main Street to the cinema and bought a bag of popcorn from Stella Brunsvold. They sat down just as the theater lights dimmed and waited for that afternoon's feature, *The Beast from 20,000 Fathoms.*

First came a Tom and Jerry cartoon, and Wes laughed so loud and hard that a few tears rolled down his cheeks. Embarrassed, Franny ducked down in her seat and peered around to see if any of her classmates were seated nearby. Fortunately, the only other moviegoer was Rodney the jail janitor, who spent more time at Hauser's than he did cleaning the town's perpetually empty prison cell.

Next came the newsreel. Franny sighed impatiently as the announcer droned on and on about Senator McCarthy, as usual.

"That man's a real stinker," said Wes, devouring a handful of dry popcorn. "He'll get his, mark my words."

"What do you mean?" asked Franny, slinking down even lower in her seat. Wes always talked too loud at the movies.

"Look at him," Wes said, pointing to the screen. "First, he said that all of Hollywood was filled with Commies, and now he's going to try to convince us that the whole U.S. Army is too. He gets people to tattle on their friends and neighbors and call them Commie spies—and nine times out of ten, it's all lies."

"How does he get them to do that?" Franny asked.

"He scares 'em," Wes said. "He tells folks that if they don't go along with his accusations and give him names of supposed Communist traitors, he'll tell everyone that they're Commies too. Make up things about suspicious behavior and that sort of thing. It's blackmail. Makes my skin crawl."

Franny thought about the odd things that had happened at Olga's house, and she wished that she could talk to her father about them. "But what if someone *is* suspicious?" she asked tentatively. "*Should* you say something to someone?"

"Only if you're absolutely sure that you've got your facts straight," Wes said, rattling the paper bag to get to the salty bits at the bottom. "Otherwise, you might just make a big mess of someone's life—and for what? Just to spread rumors."

He took another noisy bite of popcorn. "Senator McCarthy is turning this whole country into a small town, where everyone trades secrets about everyone else and no one has any privacy. I'm telling you—it makes me long for the days of the Wild West, when you could just get on a horse and ride into the sunset, without feeling like a thousand pairs of eyes were watching you. Oh, good—here comes the movie."

And with that, Wes and Franny forgot about Senator

McCarthy, suspicious behavior, and blackmail for two whole hours. Instead, they watched a film in which a nuclear bomb woke up a frozen dinosaur, which promptly stomped from the Arctic all the way to New York City and smashed up Wall Street.

Even though the movie wasn't supposed to be funny, Wes laughed all the way through it.

"Hurry up—you are late," said Olga, brusquely opening the front door and ushering Franny into the music room the following Monday. "We have a good deal to discuss today." She pointed to the velvet couch. "Please."

As Franny sat down, she searched her teacher's face for any hints of anxiety after the visit from the men in the dark car. There were none—but then again, Olga was almost always as inscrutable as the Mona Lisa. Franny glanced around, looking for the envelope with the summons, but of course, Olga had stashed it away somewhere—maybe in the bedroom or basement, or even inside one of the instruments. Franny resolved to scour the house for it when she did the chores later.

"*Dyevushka*—are you listening to me?" Olga thundered. "I have been talking for five minutes, and you are someplace else, up on a little cloud maybe. Pay attention!"

"Sorry," said Franny guiltily.

"What I was saying was this: I would like for you to enter a big contest, and—"

"Really?" Franny exclaimed, sitting straight up. "Where? At the school again?"

Olga looked most displeased. "Do not interrupt—it is very rude," she said. "As I keep *trying* to tell you: for this contest, you will go to Minneapolis and give a recital in a hall in front of several judges. About ten other pianists will compete against you. You are becoming a good musician with my help, and I think that you have a very good chance at winning."

"Minneapolis!" squawked Franny.

Minneapolis, or the Big City, as it was known to the inhabitants of Rusty Nail, was so far away that it took more than five whole hours to drive there. Franny had never been there, and her heart pounded with excitement and fear. "But I've never been in a really big contest before! Are you sure that I'm good enough? Will there be a lot of people there? Will you be there?"

"Yes, yes, and yes," Olga said. "All you must do is prepare a good deal, play your best, and wait for the judges' decision. But I must tell you this: it is a *very* important contest, and you'll play against the other best young pianists in the state. Some of them may be eighteen years old."

"Why would they even let me into the contest?" Franny asked nervously. "I'm only ten."

"Just the fact that you are my student is reason enough," said Olga. "And in any case, it is not until April, so you have more than enough time to prepare."

Franny nodded, her heart still beating at the rate of a hummingbird's—and she suddenly faltered. Playing against Nancy in front of Eunice Grimes was one thing, but a competition of this caliber was quite another.

"Do I have to?" she asked.

"Of course you do," said Olga indignantly. "All of the great pianists have played in contests—they didn't just sit around giving solo concerts. Mozart competed against Clementi in front of Emperor Joseph II. Beethoven shamed many pianists in competitions. Doing so gives you a chance to show how much better you are than all of your contemporaries. Music is an art, but anyone who tells you that it's not in part a sport would be lying to you."

"But all of those kids will be so much bigger than me," Franny said.

Olga waved her hand dismissively. "That does not mean they will be better," she said. "Talent shows itself very early, or not at all. And it is good for you to be nervous. You are training to be a performer, not a hermit who sits with her piano in a closet.

"And now I have something else to tell you," Olga continued. "I only need you to come on Wednesday, Thursday, and Friday to help me. I am taking on another student, and she will come on Mondays and Tuesdays."

Franny's nervous excitement ground to a halt. "*What* other student?" she asked, a black feeling spreading through her insides.

Just then the doorbell rang. Olga walked into the foyer

and opened the front door. And then Franny heard the following: "Hello, Mrs. Malenkov. How are you this afternoon?"

It was *Nancy Orilee.*

For a moment, Franny thought that she must be asleep and having a nightmare. Her heart pounded in her ears, and she could just barely hear Olga say in reply: "Yes, hello. Wait in the living room, please, until I am finished with my other guest." Then she marched back into the music room and closed the door. She looked at Franny.

"Now, what was your question?"

Franny sat on her hands so that Olga wouldn't see them shaking. "I asked," she managed to say, "who your other student is, but I think I know."

"Ah, Nancy is a classmate of yours?" Olga asked, seemingly oblivious to Franny's agony. "Her mother came by last week and begged me to instruct her daughter, whose usual teacher got into a bad tractor accident. He is in a full body cast and cannot drive here to see her. So, I listened to her play, and she is passable. Not brilliant—but I think that it would be good for you to have a little competition."

"She is *not* passable," Franny shouted. "She's *horrible!*"

"What is the matter with you?" Olga asked.

"Madame Malenkov," Franny pleaded. "It's not fair— I had to *beg* you for lessons, and she just sails in and gets them too!"

"Nonsense!" Olga said. "She too would work. I said that already."

"It's still not fair!" yelled Franny. "*Please* don't teach her! She's the meanest girl in the whole town. She's always putting me and Sandy down, and she thinks she's so much better than everyone else because her dad is rich. And every time something good happens to me, she finds a way to ruin it. And now she's going to ruin my lessons with you. Please don't teach her!" And with that, she started to cry.

"That is *enough*," Olga commanded. "You are acting like a child. You had better get used to having rivals, because *every* pianist has them. This is precisely one of the reasons I am taking Nancy on as a student—to make you realize that you are not the only one out there who has hopes and ambitions. If you are too much of a child to face that, then you are too much of a child to be under my instruction. And just so you know, I am going to enroll Nancy in the contest as well."

Franny felt like an arrow had been shot through her heart.

"Then I *quit*!" she shouted.

"You *what*?" said Olga.

"Quit!" Franny yelled. "It's not fair. I always stick up for you in town when everyone calls you a Commie, and I keep all of your secrets—like not being able to answer the phone and—" She stopped herself before she mentioned the men on the porch, but couldn't help blurting out: "And then you go and stab me in the back!"

Olga's face reddened with anger and she pointed to the door. "You go home right now," she said. "Do not come back until you are ready to apologize to me. I have never heard such rudeness—never! Out with you!"

Franny snatched up her bag and music books and yanked the music-room door open. On her way out, she saw Nancy Orilee waiting primly in the living room.

"I *hate* you!" Franny yelled viciously, and ran out of the house.

She didn't stop running until she got home.

Chapter Sixteen

"What are you doing home?" asked Lorraine in surprise when Franny trudged into the apartment the next day after school. "Why aren't you at Madame Malenkov's house?"

"She said that she didn't need any help today," Franny lied. At supper the night before, Wes had looked so cheerful under his eyeshade that Franny simply hadn't had the heart to tell her family that she'd quit her lessons.

"Oh," said Lorraine. "In that case, why don't you help me in the kitchen. I'm making *rommegrot*."

Ugh, Franny thought. *Rommegrot* was a Norwegian pudding made from cream and flour, and Lorraine's version always resembled a vat of lumpy, colorless paste. Also, it required thankless hours of stirring.

"I was going to take my bike out to see Sandy," she said quickly. "I haven't seen her in a real long time, because of all the lessons and practicing." She tried very hard to look pitiful and deprived of social contact. In fact, Franny hadn't told her parents that Sandy had been snubbing her. It was just too embarrassing to involve them in her social life on top of everything else.

"Go ahead," Lorraine said, walking back into the kitchen to do battle with the pudding. "Just be back in time for supper."

Franny left and retrieved her bike from the shed in the alley behind her building. She hadn't been out to Sandy's farmhouse in a long time. The trip on the road through the cornfields seemed to take forever, and Franny's lungs burned from breathing in the cold, late-November air. The prospect of confronting Sandy made Franny terribly nervous, but with no one to discuss the Olga ordeal with, Franny missed her friend more than ever. She was determined to mend the rift.

At last, the Hellickson farm came into sight on the horizon. Franny parked her bike in the driveway and knocked on the back door. Sandy's older brother, Lowell, opened it.

"Well, look-y who we've got here," he said, smiling wryly. "The Commie-in-training."

"Be quiet," snapped Franny. "Is Sandy here?"

"She's still grounded," Lowell said benevolently. "But

if you give me a nickel, I'll tell you where you can find her."

"All I've got is a penny," Franny said, digging it out of her pocket.

"That'll do," Lowell said, taking it. He pointed at the garage. "She's in there, buildin' somethin'. See you later, Comrade." He closed the door.

Franny scowled and marched across the backyard, the frozen grass crunching under her shoes. She reached the garage and tentatively knocked on the door, her heart pounding.

"Who is it?" called Sandy.

"It's me," said Franny. She pushed the door open and walked inside.

Sandy had been standing over some sort of awkward, boxlike contraption and hammering a crooked old nail into its side. She froze when she saw Franny.

"What're you doin' here?"

"I came to tell you that I quit taking piano lessons," Franny said.

"Oh," said Sandy, turning her attention back to the box. "Why? I thought that playin' the piano with the Commie was the most important thing in the world to you. More important than your friends and everything else."

"I just didn't want to do it anymore," Franny said, kicking at the ground.

Sandy looked at her friend suspiciously. "I don't believe you," she said. "Somethin' must've happened. I bet
Olga gave you the boot, and then you thought that you'd
come by and say hi to ole Sandy, now that you had nothin'
better to do."

"She didn't give me the boot," said Franny. "I'm tired
of us being in a fight, so I came out here to talk to you.
What're you making?"

"It's gonna be a car," Sandy said. "Lowell said he'd
help me put a motor in it and everythin'. And don't go
tryin' to change the subject, by the way. I've known you
your whole life, and I know that you didn't just quit out
of the blue."

"Fine," Franny caved in. "I quit because Olga started
teaching Nancy Orilee too."

Sandy gasped. "What! Why? Didn't you tell her what a
worm Prancy is?"

"I tried," Franny said, and she told Sandy all about the
contest and her fight with Olga the day before. "And after
all I've done for her! Sticking up for her and stuff, and
risking making everyone in town hate me as much as they
hate her." She stopped to take a breath. "Anyway, aren't
you glad that I quit? Now we'll have all of our afternoons
together again, just like the old days."

Sandy shook her head. "You got it wrong this time,
Franny," she said. "You know that, don't you?"

"What do you mean?"

"I mean this: you're the one who's gonna be sorry you quit, not Olga. How're you gonna get famous if she doesn't help you? Use your head, for Pete's sake."

"Didn't you *hear* me?" Franny exclaimed. "She's teaching *Nancy Orilee*. The worst girl in the world. How could I stick around after she did that to me?"

"This is why you should stick around," said Sandy. "You've gotta get back in there and fight—and beat Nancy Orilee once and for all. It changes *everythin'* now that Prancy's in the mix. Don't you see? You've got a *real* chance to lick her once and for all. If you win that contest, you'll show everyone that you're the best pianist in the state. The queen of Rusty Nail's gonna lose her throne— to you!"

"But I don't even think Olga would take me back now, after some of the things I said to her," Franny said, her resolve faltering. "About being a backstabber and all."

"You said that to her?" Sandy cringed. "Oh well— never mind. You gotta think like a boxer. Those guys don't lie down after one punch. We've got the most important round ahead of us now. Or else you're gonna get left behind, just like your dad did."

"What do you mean, *we* have the most important round ahead of us?" Franny asked. "First you don't talk to me for weeks 'cause I took lessons with Olga, and now you want me to go *back* and work even harder than before? I don't get it."

Sandy sat down on her box and blew her hair out of her eyes. "Sure, I was mad," she said. "I'm still mad. You hurt my feelin's real bad, leavin' me out like that. How'd you like to get left out and left behind?"

"I'm really sorry," Franny said solemnly. "I didn't mean to leave you out."

"Better apologize like you mean it," Sandy said.

"I'm sorry!" yelled Franny, tears burning the corners of her eyes. "I'll never do it again. You're my best friend, and I need your help figuring out what to do."

"Aw, quit bawlin'," Sandy said, looking satisfied now. "I *guess* I can forgive you and help you out." She looked at Franny slyly. "If you gimme back Old Blue."

Franny blinked. "You mean that dumb marble?" she asked, wiping her eyes. "Fine—it's yours." Suddenly things seemed like they were going to be okay.

"Lo-o-o-ord—you're actin' like such a girl!" Sandy exclaimed. "If you want me to help you, you'd better pull yourself together. And you have to buy candy for me at the five-and-dime, since I'm still officially grounded."

"Deal," said Franny, wiping her cheeks.

"Now let's go inside. I'm freezing," Sandy said, wiping her filthy hands on her trousers. "Wanna stay for supper?"

Franny nodded, grateful to escape the *rommegrot* waiting for her back home. The girls walked back through the chilly air to the house, still a little shy and awkward around each other after their long falling-out.

But if Franny had any doubts about Sandy's feelings and loyalty, they vanished the next day after school. Sandy walked to Olga's house with her and waited patiently in the peony bush while Franny went inside and apologized to Olga.

It was time for the contest to begin.

Part III
Allegro

Chapter Seventeen

Franny usually loved Rusty Nail's winters more than any other season. Year after year, the town became a splendid warren of shoveled paths in snow sometimes three or four feet deep. The men took their trucks over to the frozen Mississippi River, cut holes in the ice, and fished like Eskimos. A comforting assortment of sleds, damp mittens, and rubber boots littered the stairwell leading up to the Hansens' apartment.

This year, however, the season flashed by so quickly that Franny barely even noticed the wintry activities going on around her. She practiced all the time, getting ready for the contest. Naturally, this nearly drove Owen and Jessie crazy. Things nearly got out of hand one January afternoon.

The boys came home before supper as Franny was practicing a particularly tricky part of a Chopin piece.

Owen kicked off his snow-covered boots, which clattered noisily down the front stairs. "Mo-om!" he shouted. "When's supper?"

There was a typical crash from the kitchen. "Ohhh," cried Lorraine. "Not just yet."

Jessie switched on the radio and turned up the volume. "Good—we're just in time for the show," he said as *The Colgate Sports Newsreel* blared out of the speakers.

"Turn that off!" Franny yelled. "I can't concentrate! It's loud as a tractor!"

"Aw, turn yourself off," said Owen. "You think we want to hear the same song over and over again, like a broken record?"

"Yeah," added Jessie. "You think you're the only one who lives here? You're not a star yet, so you can stop actin' like one." And he turned up the radio even louder.

"Mom!" shrieked Franny. "Make them turn down the radio! They're trying to ruin my practicing for the contest! If I don't win, it will be all their fault!"

Finally, the shouting grew so loud that Wes clambered up the stairs from his office to see what was going on. He solved the problem at last by dragging the twanging piano into Franny's bedroom.

That night, Franny lay in her bed and stared at the piano as it glistened in the moonlight. She watched the reflection of the Main Street traffic light flicker on the right side of the instrument. Green, yellow, red. Green, yellow, red. In Franny's mind, the changing colors translated into an endless three-note song.

In fact, that whole winter, she started experiencing the entire world around her in terms of music more than ever.

When she heard Mrs. Charity Engebraten's mangy little terrier barking up the street, *staccato* came to Franny's mind, a word that meant crisp, short, and detached sounds. Each night, she listened to her father's deep, even snores down the hallway and thought: *legato,* or notes played in a smooth, connected, and flowing manner. Lorraine was *dolce,* which meant sweet and soft. Sandy always reminded her of *brio,* or lively and spirited. And Olga, of course, evoked *maestoso*—music played with majesty and grandeur.

And when she was actually at a piano, whether at Olga's grand Steinway or the upright in her own bedroom, nothing else mattered to Franny besides the music. Her life itself was in a state of *crescendo*—a passage played with a steady increase in intensity or force. She didn't know yet just what it was all building up to—but Franny was quite aware that her place and purpose in the world was changing forever.

Sandy assumed the unofficial role of Franny's coach.

"Now, I don't want you to pay a lick of attention to your competitor," she advised. "Just keep your eye on the prize, Franny. But don't you worry: I'll bother Prancy for both of us."

Then she came up with three ways to distract Nancy from preparing for the contest:

1. Release termites into Nancy's piano at home.
2. Steal Nancy's mittens as often as possible so that her fingers would freeze and fall off, hence reducing her ability to play the piano.
3. Create disturbances outside Olga's music-room window during Nancy's lesson.

Since termites were hard to come by and stealing was against the law, Franny and Sandy decided that #3 was their only real option.

So, one afternoon, Sandy camped out in the snow-covered peony bush during Nancy's lesson time and did noisy imitations of the American coot's mating call. Olga responded by simply opening the window and dumping a glass of water on Sandy, who fled the scene.

"I *told* you, Franny," Sandy said afterward. She'd run straight to Franny's house after the incident, her face red with frost and little icicles dangling from her scarf and hat. "The pranks just don't work anymore. Go over to that piano and practice some more. We've gotta beat her at her own game."

On a Friday afternoon in late March, not long before the competition, Franny walked over to Olga's house for her lesson. Charlie was away on yet another long work trip, and Franny had been helping Olga more than usual with her errands and cleaning.

It was unusually mild that day, and the front door had been left open to let in the fresh early-spring breezes.

Franny knocked on the screen door and waited. No one answered. To her surprise, she heard voices coming from the kitchen. It sounded like Olga had another lady in there with her!

That's weird, Franny thought. Olga never had guests over. She knocked again, but the ladies didn't hear her. Overcome by curiosity, Franny gathered her courage, let herself in, and sidled up the hallway toward the kitchen.

As she got closer, she realized that Olga was speaking in *Russian* to her guest, which clearly meant that this was no run-of-the-mill Rusty Nail coffee visit. The women were arguing noisily, and Franny's heart raced as she eavesdropped. Of course, she couldn't understand a single word of what they were saying, until the guest said in heavily accented English: "*Nyet!* That is enough, Olga!

Hiding is for cowards! You must decide what you are going to do!"

And they lapsed back into Russian again. Franny leaned in toward the doorway as far as she dared, trying to get a peek at the visitor. To her horror, the floorboard under her feet creaked as she shifted her weight. The conversation in the kitchen halted.

"*Dyevushka?* Is that you?" called Olga.

Franny meekly tiptoed into the room. "I just got here," she said, red faced. "The front door was open."

She stared at the visitor, whose appearance astonished her. Heavy and coarse as a big potato, the woman had meaty, liver-spot-covered hands and frizzy gray hair that stuck out in every direction. Who on earth *was* she? She certainly couldn't be a friend of Olga's, Franny reasoned, for she wasn't nearly elegant enough. She decided that Olga must have imported a maid or something from back home.

"It is good that you can play the piano," Olga said. "Because you could never earn a living as a spy. *Dyevushka,* this is Svetlana. Svetlana, this is the girl I told you about."

"Hello," Franny said, still staring at the guest in fascination. The woman just nodded at Franny and slurped from her coffee cup.

Olga stood up. "All right—it is time for your lesson," she said, briskly ushering Franny out of the room.

"Madame Malenkov," Franny whispered to Olga when they were safely in the music room. "Who is that lady?"

"Svetlana is visiting with me for a while," Olga responded vaguely. "As you might have guessed, she is a Russian like me. Oh, excuse me—I meant to say 'Commie,' " she added, smirking. "Please begin with the Chopin."

Franny sat at the piano. *Oh boy,* she thought. *If the Colosseum women find out that another Russian's in town, they're going to go crazy!* She spread her music out on the piano and began to play, although she could barely concentrate on the notes in front of her.

Olga stood over Franny impatiently.

"The timing is not quite right," she said. "Try it one more time. . . . That's better. The tone should be richer. Try it yet again."

Just then, Svetlana lumbered in and heaved herself down on the settee. She gave out a pulpy, rasping cough. Franny looked up at Olga, expecting her to shoo the maid out of the room. To her surprise, Olga only looked down at her and said: "Well? What are you waiting for, *Dyevushka*—a special invitation? Start over, please."

Franny resumed her playing. Just as she got to the second page of the piece, Svetlana blew her nose with the might of a foghorn. Franny leaped up off the bench.

"*Now* what?" Olga asked irritably. "Keep going." It took another ten minutes before Olga was satisfied with the phrase. They moved on to Mozart.

Just as she reached a particularly sweet and intricate part of her piece, Franny heard another annoying noise come from the settee area. Svetlana was scratching her thigh with great zest, as though her pants leg contained itchy straw. Franny lost her concentration and made a mistake.

"What happened?" Olga said. "You played that perfectly last week. Play it again."

Svetlana hacked again, and gave one more noisy scratch for good measure—but after that, she quieted down long enough for Franny to get through the piece without mistakes.

"Very good," Olga said. "Make sure that you do not rush the middle part. You are always in a hurry to get to the end. And now play the Liszt."

Franny put the music up in front of her and played. Suddenly she heard a new noise coming from behind her. At first, she thought it was an odd, droning alarm somewhere off in the distance—was it an air-raid siren? Her stomach flip-flopped, and then she realized that it was only Svetlana, humming along to the music. Franny looked up at her teacher and raised her eyebrows indignantly.

"*Now* what?" said Olga, clearly annoyed.

"She's *humming*," Franny said under her breath, jerking her head in the direction of the settee. "I can't concentrate."

"If you are going to perform in big concert halls, you had better get used to distractions," Olga said matter-of-factly. Then she said something to Svetlana in Russian, and both ladies laughed.

Franny's face burned red as she pounded through the

rest of the lesson. First of all, she couldn't believe that Olga would allow this oafish stranger to sit in on one of her lessons. But to do so right before the most important contest of her life? Franny didn't know what to think. And the fact that Olga and Svetlana had shared an inside joke, probably at her expense, only infuriated her even more.

"My, you are playing with such passion this evening," Olga said mischievously. "The judges will be very impressed."

Svetlana blew her nose again noisily. Franny glared at her over her shoulder.

"I have a bad cold," the woman explained. "This town is like Siberia." And then, to Olga: "Next time you hide out, do it in Hawaii, *da*?"

If you hate it so much, why don't you go back to Russia again, stinky old Svetlana, Franny thought, glowering. Anyway, why was Olga letting the maid talk to her like that? If Franny had ever been sassy, Olga would have sent her from the house.

"Okay, *Dyevushka,* the lesson is over now," Olga said hurriedly. "I would like you to pay special attention to the tone of the Mozart. It is not quite there—but almost. Just remember that Mozart is always light and clean, like springtime. He always insisted on naturalness, and so do I. See you again next week."

Franny snatched her music books off the piano and

gave Svetlana one last stare before she stomped out into the snow.

The following Monday, when Franny arrived at school, a large group of kids stood huddled near the front door. As she approached them, Franny heard Sandy's voice calling out from the middle of the mob: "Three to one—Franny Hansen versus Prancy Orilee. Those are the odds, folks. Take it or leave it. It'll be the contest of a lifetime."

Franny pushed her way into the center of the circle, where Sandy was the main attraction. She held a jar of coins and a pad and pencil. Just then, Runty dropped a dime in the jar and said: "Ten cents on Franny."

Sandy scribbled down:

10¢, Runty, on FH

"Sandy—what on earth are you *doing*?" Franny asked.

"Whaddya think? Startin' a betting pool on the piano contest," Sandy said. "Just to get your morale up. Guess what—everyone's pullin' for you, and we have almost three whole dollars of bets. And that's before recess even."

Franny's face reddened as she pulled Sandy aside.

"But what if I lose and Nancy wins?" she asked. "Have you thought about that? Everyone will hate me."

"Aw, you won't lose," said Sandy breezily. "Everyone

heard you play at the Eunice Grimes concert, and we all know you're better than ole Prancy-pants. Soon the whole world will know it."

Franny's throat squeezed in anxiety. Without saying another word, she walked into Miss Hamm's classroom, sat down, and took deep breaths. All morning, she stared at the back of Nancy's golden head and hoped that Nancy had jitters as well. *Probably not,* Franny concluded grimly. *Prancy's got nerves of steel, and a heart to match.* To distract herself, she ran through her contest pieces in her mind over and over again.

At one point, Sandy turned around to her and whispered: "Hey, Franny, cut it out. That's real annoyin'."

"Cut what out?" asked Franny, surprised.

"You keep drumming your fingers on the desk, like you're playing the piano. Everyone keeps looking at you."

Franny blinked. "I didn't realize that I was doing that," she said, looking around in embarrassment. She sat on her hands for the rest of the week to keep herself from doing it again.

Finally, Friday arrived, the last day before the contest. After the morning bell rang, Sandy hovered outside the classroom as everyone else filed in.

"*Now* what are you doing?" Franny asked Sandy from the cloakroom. "You're going to be late."

"You'll see," Sandy whispered excitedly. "Go sit down."

"Just don't get us in trouble," Franny said nervously,

and she went into the classroom and took her seat. Nancy Orilee flounced into the room and sat down, preciously arranging the ruffles in her skirt around her.

Just as Miss Hamm started taking attendance, Sandy strolled in and took off her cardigan. She wore a T-shirt proclaiming in handwritten red marker:

Franny Hansen
State Piano Champion, 1954

She paraded across the front of the room so that everyone could see her. Then she turned around so that everyone could see the back of the shirt, which declared:

Last Place for Prancy

Everyone snickered, and Runty Knutson said, "Amen!" very loudly. Franny's heart pounded with affection for her friend.

Nancy Orilee stood up and yelled: "Miss Hamm! You're not going to let Sandy Anne wear that shirt today, are you?"

Miss Hamm wrung her hands. "Oh dear, oh dear," she said. "Sandy, I think you should put on your sweater."

"But it's *hot* in here," Sandy shouted. "It must be a thousand degrees. And besides, there's no dress code at the Polk School. That's disqualification."

"You mean *discrimination*," Franny corrected her in a whisper.

"Yeah—that," said Sandy. She smiled smugly at Nancy.

Miss Hamm was about to emit another round of *Oh dears* when Mr. Moody began to speak over the intercom.

"Good morning," he said wrathfully. "Someone has scribbled some profanity in chalk on the school dumpster. Once I identify the perpetrator, not only will he have to wash the whole dumpster, he'll have detention for the rest of his life."

Runty Knutson looked at the floor innocently.

"Secondly, I have an important announcement to make," Mr. Moody continued. Franny could practically see the cigarette smoke wafting out of the intercom box on the wall.

"This weekend, fifth graders Nancy Orilee and Franny Hansen are once again representing Rusty Nail with their musical talents," he said. "They'll both be playing in a contest in Minneapolis against the finest young pianists in the state. Please wish them luck if you see them in the hallways."

"Good luck, Nancy!" Runty suddenly shouted at the top of his lungs, and then let out a terribly noisy fart. The rest of the children shrieked with laughter.

"Ohhh," wailed Miss Hamm. "Runty, please go to the principal's office."

"Do I have to?" Runty said.

"Yes, please," said Miss Hamm apologetically.

"Aw, man," said Runty as he slid off his chair and stumped out of the room. When he left, Miss Hamm let out a sigh of relief and faced the class.

"Now, I think it would be very nice if we gave a little round of applause to encourage Nancy and Franny before they leave for Minneapolis," she pleaded.

All of the students clapped, and Sandy stood up and whooped a few times in Franny's direction.

Franny's fingers tingled with nervous excitement. She looked over at Nancy, who gave her a big sugary smile. Then, as the applause died down, Nancy leaned back and whispered to Franny: "*You're* going to come in last, not me. I don't know why you're even bothering to go at all."

To Franny's surprise, instead of being stung by Nancy's comment, she felt a sense of calmness wash over her. All of a sudden, she had a premonition that she was going to win. Just like that. People like Nancy Orilee always got what they deserved, and it was simply time for her rival's comeuppance. Nancy must have sensed this by the change in Franny's expression. Her smirk wilted, and she began to look unsure of herself.

At that moment, Franny knew that she had already begun to conquer Nancy Orilee.

Chapter Eighteen

The sun hadn't even risen yet when Lorraine woke Franny up the morning of the contest. Franny groggily brushed her teeth and stared at herself in the mirror. She'd spent much of the night before lying awake, thinking through every note in her music and drumming out the Mozart and Chopin pieces on her blanket over and over again.

"Here you go, honey," Lorraine said, coming into the bathroom and shaking out the "Dorothy" dress that Franny had worn to the Eunice Grimes concert. "I washed it for you last night."

"Not again!" Franny wailed. Then she noticed something, and her heart gave a hopeful little leap. "Hey—it looks funny. Is something wrong with it?"

Lorraine examined the garment with concern. "I don't think so," she said falteringly. "What do you mean?"

Franny stepped into the dress, pulled it up over her shoulders, and tried to zip it up. She was thrilled to discover that the dress was at least three sizes too small. "Mom—you shrunk it in the wash!" she shouted gleefully.

"You're kidding!" Lorraine said. She gave the zipper several hard yanks, and it tore out of the dress. "Ohhh! I don't believe it! Isn't that just my luck!"

Ho, ho, thought Franny happily. *That's a lucky break.* This was as good an omen as she could have hoped for. She ran into her bedroom and pulled on the perfectly normal-looking skirt and shirt that she'd been planning to wear all along.

A pale gray light washed the eastern sky as she and her parents drove out of Rusty Nail in their old Chevrolet. All of the houses looked dark and solemn in the early-dawn shadows. Franny half envied the other kids sleeping snugly in their warm beds behind the closed curtains and shades. Soon they'd wake up to the certainty of eggs and bacon and Saturday-morning radio shows while Franny's fate was determined many miles away in a strange city.

The car ride to Minneapolis would be the longest trip Franny had ever taken. The farthest she'd ever been before was a visit to her aunt Lillian and uncle Gustave's house in Decorah, Iowa, just an hour away. She took a deep breath and opened up one of her music books. For many minutes and miles, she just looked at the first page, not really seeing the notes at all. Wes looked at his daughter in the rearview mirror.

"Don't worry, Mozart," he said. "Just go in there and do the best that you can. No one can ask more than that, can they?"

Then he turned on the radio and found a station playing a Glenn Miller song. Wes sang along quietly to the music:

> *Standing there alone by the ashes*
> *Of the fire we said would never die . . .*
> *Will I ever find an ember*
> *Burning from the days gone by . . . ?*

He stopped singing and looked back at Franny again. "But you know what? I'm sure you're going to win. I've got a hunch. You're going to stomp Nancy Orilee into the ground, and all of those other kids too."

"We-es," said Lorraine. "That's not exactly the sort of attitude you should be encouraging."

"I speak the truth, my darling wife," Wes said sassily. "I just know that my girl's the best out there. Oh yes, she is." And he hummed along until the song dissolved into static.

Franny gave up on reading her music and watched the cornfields whiz past. She wondered how many cornstalks grew there every year. Ten thousand? A million? Ten million? The fields stretched to the horizon on both sides of the car. Eventually, Franny grew drowsy and fell into an uneasy sleep.

She woke with a start when her father yelled from the front seat: "Lorraine! You're reading that map *upside down*! No wonder we're lost! Give me that."

They had arrived in Minneapolis. Wes parked on the side of a busy street to study the map while Lorraine giggled with embarrassment. Franny sat up and rolled down the window. She had never seen so many cars or people all in one place. Everyone was in such a hurry, as opposed to in Rusty Nail, where both time and people seemed to move to the slow tempo of growing wheat.

"Oh, for Pete's sake, Lorraine," Wes bellowed. "We're on the wrong side of the city entirely, and it's already one-fifteen." According to the contest schedule, Franny was to play for the judges shortly after three o'clock.

"Oops," said Lorraine sheepishly. "Well, at least we know where we are now. Can we stop at that gas station over there? I need to use the ladies' room."

"Mo-om!" Franny wailed in the backseat. "We're going to miss the contest! Can't you hold it?"

"No, I can't," said Lorraine crossly while Wes yelled at Franny not to yell at her mother. They nearly caused a four-car accident as Wes pulled the Chevrolet into rushing traffic. Several drivers honked at him.

"What's your hurry, fellas?" he shouted out the window.

"Boy, people are impatient up here," he added as a chorus of angry car horns filled the air.

It was almost two o'clock when they finally arrived at a gigantic yellow-brick university hall, the site of the competition. After cruising around the building three times, Wes parked the car illegally in front of it, and Lorraine and Franny ran inside.

After following dozens of paper arrows posted around the maze of hallways, Franny saw Olga waiting impatiently outside the main auditorium.

"You are late, *Dyevushka*," she said, scowling. "I thought that perhaps you changed your mind about coming."

To Franny's enormous annoyance, she saw dowdy old Svetlana standing behind Olga, reading papers on a notice board. Why had Olga brought *her* to the competition?

"Ohhh," said Lorraine. "We're late because of me. We had a . . . a problem with the map. I'm Lorraine Hansen, Franny's mother. It's so nice to finally meet you—I've heard so much about you around town."

An embarrassing silence followed this last blundering comment. But then Olga broke the tension with a small, formal smile.

"Yes, it is very nice to meet you too," she said. "Frances resembles you."

That's right, Franny thought. *They've never met before!* It seemed impossible to her that the two most important women in her life had never overlapped, even in a town as minuscule as Rusty Nail.

"Ugh," said Svetlana to no one in particular. She was examining a roster of contestants. "I hope that nobody plays Bach—so dreary."

"You must practice a little before you play," Olga said to Franny brusquely. "Come with me."

She swept down the hallway. Franny trailed after her, leaving her mother to make awkward small talk with Svetlana.

Olga led Franny into a little room that contained nothing but an old, scuffed upright piano and a plastic chair. Olga flipped a switch on the wall, and a dingy fluorescent light flickered on overhead.

"I know it is boring, but I think you should play some scales to get your hands and fingers warmed up," said Olga.

Franny scraped the plastic chair over to the piano and flexed her fingers. Starting in C major, she began to play, up and down three octaves. Then she stopped.

"Madame Malenkov, why did you bring Svetlana to the competition?" she said, trying to sound casual. "And why did you let her sit in on my lessons?"

"Why—did that make you nervous?" Olga asked.

"I guess so." Franny resisted the urge to tell Olga how vexing the Russian visitor had been, with all of her scratching, coughing, and humming.

"That's good, *Dyevushka,*" Olga said. "As I keep telling you, it is good for you to learn how to play the piano while you are nervous. All fine performers must learn how to play under enormous pressure. And audiences can be so annoying."

"Do you think that *I'm* a fine performer?" Franny asked, fishing for a compliment.

"We will find out today," said Olga, and then she smiled gently. "Let me put it to you this way: I think that you are a fine pianist and could become a great one. Why else would I spend so much of my time teaching you? Do I seem like the kind of person who likes to waste her time and energy?"

"No," said Franny, nearly blushing. "But I had to work hard to get you to teach me in the first place, you know."

"Yes, that is true," Olga said. "But all things that are worth having are also hard to get. I am proud of your determination to overcome the odds. It is very impressive for such a young girl."

They practiced until it was nearly time for Franny's performance. She took a deep breath and followed Olga out into the hallway.

Just then, Franny saw Nancy Orilee come out of a practice room down the corridor.

"How was the warming up?" asked Olga.

"Perfect," said Nancy. "I'm all ready." She looked over at Franny smugly.

"Hurry up, then," Olga said. "Judges hate latecomers. Nancy—you play at three. And Franny, you go at three-twenty. You've both worked hard and this is your big moment. Now go show the judges that there is nothing small-town about you girls when it comes to playing the piano.

"Oh," she added as she walked down the hallway. "*Oudachi*. That means 'good luck' in Russian."

Franny and Nancy met their families outside the auditorium and went inside to find seats. Franny had never been in such a grand room. Dark wood paneling covered the walls, and thick, plush, red-velvet curtains framed the stage. Several photographers loitered at the foot of the stage, and one of them set up a heavy tripod.

"Look at that," said Wes, pointing it out to Franny as they took their seats. "Do you know what that's for? A television camera! Look—the case has a CBS sticker on it! Whaddya think of that, Mozart! Your genius is going to be immortalized on film!"

Olga and Svetlana stayed in the back and talked to each other in Russian. The Orilees sat across the room from Franny and her family. Makeup spackled every inch of Mrs. Orilee's face, and she dabbed some bright raspberry gloss onto Nancy's lips.

Franny rolled and unrolled her music in her hands. About ten other contestants sat in the auditorium with their families. As Olga had promised, some of the pianists looked about seventeen or eighteen years old.

Then the three judges came into the room. As they

walked down the main aisle, Mr. Orilee rose and marched up to them, shaking each of their hands assertively. They all began a quiet but animated discussion.

Wes eyed them suspiciously.

"Looks like Roger Orilee's pretty chummy with those judges," he said darkly. "I wonder what he's up to. I've never trusted that man, not since we were in kindergarten together."

The judges finally walked up onto the stage, where they sat in a row like three crows on a wire.

"Welcome to Minneapolis, contestants," announced one of them. "My name is Mr. Pilskog, and I'm the head of the judging committee." He nodded toward his colleagues and added: "This is Mr. Fauskanger and Mr. Skadberg."

The other two judges nodded sternly and took out their pads and pencils.

"When we call your name, please come up onto the stage and start playing immediately. Each contestant will play two pieces. We'll announce the winner in an assembly here at eight o'clock. Good luck to everyone, and let's begin. Now, who's first? Nancy Orilee of Rusty Nail!"

Nancy's parents clapped as she flounced up onto the stage. She curtsied to the judges and set up her music.

"Welcome, my dear. You're playing Schubert and Brahms, right?" asked Mr. Pilskog, looking at his list.

"Yes, sir," Nancy said, and gave the judges a big beauty-queen smile.

"We're looking forward to it," said Mr. Pilskog.

Nancy gave her skirt one last little ruffle and began to play. Franny listened critically. Sandy had been right when she said that Nancy sounded like a player piano. Her music had no *feeling,* and she played like a robot. To Franny, Nancy's recital was like listening to someone make an exciting story into a dull sermon.

"That girl might as well be playing a typewriter," whispered someone in the row behind Franny.

"Maybe she's better in private than she is onstage," answered somebody else. "Poor thing."

Ha ha! Franny thought jubilantly. *So I'm not the only one who hears how boring she is! Prancy's going to lose!* Even though there were eight other contestants to worry about, Nancy's delicious mediocrity filled Franny with confidence. She wished that Sandy and Runty could have witnessed this long-overdue downfall.

Soon Nancy began her second piece. Franny turned her attention to the judges, expecting them to appear as unimpressed as the rest of the audience—but instead, they were watching attentively. Mr. Fauskanger even smiled encouragingly at Nancy and nodded.

"Dad!" Franny whispered urgently. "Why do you think the judges are being so nice to Nancy? She's nothing special—everyone can hear that!"

Wes put his arm around his daughter. "They're probably nice to all the contestants, to make them less nervous. Don't worry—you're going to blow her out of the water."

"Shh!" someone hissed behind them.

Finally, Nancy plunked her way through her finale. She stood up and bowed to the judges, who beamed at her. The audience clapped politely as she collected her music and pranced down the stage stairs, where her parents cooed and petted her.

"Next!" called out Mr. Pilskog. "Frances Hansen, also of Rusty Nail!"

Franny shot up out of her chair and charged up the stage stairs.

"Knock 'em dead, Mozart," called Wes in a loud whisper. Franny cringed with embarrassment.

"What are you playing again?" asked Mr. Pilskog indifferently, leafing through his papers and not even looking in her direction.

"A Mozart variation in C major and Chopin's Etude in C Minor," Franny said.

"Go ahead, then," said Mr. Pilskog. "Start with the Mozart."

Franny sat down at the piano and arranged her music in front of her. The greedy determination that she'd first felt during the Eunice Grimes concert came back to her, and she couldn't resist sneaking a defiant look at Nancy.

"Whenever you're ready," said Mr. Skadberg.

Franny closed her eyes and took a deep breath. In her imagination, the room around her began to shift and change, and so did the people in it, like a dream. Crystal chandeliers unfurled like vines down from the ceiling, and in the wall lamps, candles appeared where lightbulbs had once been rooted in their sockets. Fine dresses and whalebone corsets wrapped themselves around the ladies in the audience, and powdered wigs fluttered down upon their neat modern hairdos. The men no longer wore modest cotton button-downs, but instead donned fine waistcoats and shirts with cascades of ruffles down the front. In her imagination, Franny wasn't sitting in Minneapolis in 1954 but in Vienna in the 1700s, about to play for a royal court—like Mozart himself.

She put her hands on the keyboard and began to perform. The music filled her mind, and Franny's notes were clean and light as crisp morning air. Her timing was perfect all the way through to the end of the piece, like a clear stream that rushes here and lulls there. She played the last notes with great flourish and pushed back from the piano in triumph. The audience clapped enthusiastically.

"Go ahead with the second piece, Miss Hansen," said Mr. Fauskanger impatiently.

Franny immediately searched the crowd for Olga's face. The Russian nodded in encouragement, and Franny's heart pounded proudly in her chest as she put her hands on the keyboard again.

She began playing the Chopin. The music was very different from the first piece. While light and hope filled Mozart's music, the Chopin piece was darker, trickier. Franny felt like she was having conversations with two very different people. She smiled impishly to herself as she navigated the hard parts, as though answering Chopin's riddles and leaping over hurdles. When she finished at last, she pushed the piano bench back again. As the audience applauded, she stood up to face the judges and waited for their praise to pour over her.

"Thank you, Miss Hansen," Mr. Pilskog said rather dully. "Next! Astrid Arnbjorg of New Ulm."

And that was *it:* the most important moment of Franny's young life had only lasted twenty minutes, and ended with such little fanfare! In a state of disbelief, Franny walked down the stairs and sat with her family.

The last of the contestants finished at seven o'clock. Everyone stampeded out of the auditorium and milled around nervously, waiting for the judges to make up their minds.

"You were definitely the best one there," said Wes, stretching. "I don't even know why they called it a contest, when the winner was so obvious from the very beginning. This is *it,* baby girl! Now I'm going to check on the car."

Just then, Olga and Svetlana walked up to Franny and Lorraine.

"You played very well, *Dyevushka,*" Olga said. "I am very confident that you will win."

"Really?" said Franny happily. "Do you really think that?"

"Yes," said the Russian. "The Mozart was perfect, and judges love that piece. I used to play it for all of my competitions. In fact, it was one of the first things I learned at Juilliard."

"Juilliard?" asked Lorraine. "Where's that?"

Olga looked shocked at the question, but then composed herself. "The Juilliard School in New York City is the best music school in the country, if not the world," she said. "I began when I was fourteen years old and stayed until I was sixteen."

"Fourteen years old!" Lorraine exclaimed. "Goodness! Isn't that awfully young?"

"Certainly not," said Olga. "In fact, I was embarrassed by how old I was when I got there. All great pianists are prodigies. Mozart went on his first tour when he was six years old. Many of them have written concertos and symphonies by the age of ten. Luckily, there was someone there who was still willing to take me on at Juilliard—a master who gives me brushup sessions even today."

"Really!" said Lorraine uneasily.

"Yes," said Olga. "Naturally, it did not take me long to catch up, and I began performing almost immediately. But I hardly consider myself a prodigy, as all of the newspaper articles say about me."

Svetlana blew her nose. "You had other things on your mind when you were very young," she interjected phlegmily. "Like survival."

Olga nodded solemnly. "Yes, that is true. Now please

excuse me." And she walked down the hallway, with Svetlana shuffling along at her side.

Lorraine smoothed down Franny's hair. "Fourteen years old," she said quietly, shaking her head. "Call me old-fashioned, but it just doesn't seem right to end one's childhood so early." And she seized her daughter's hand protectively.

Time slowed down to a crawl as they waited for the awards assembly. Wes ambled back to his family after making sure that no one had stolen their ancient Chevy. Franny sat with her parents on rickety plastic chairs in the hallway and watched the second hand circle the face of a yellowing old wall clock in the hall. Around and around it went, ten times, twenty times, sixty times.

"All right, Mozart," said Wes just before eight, playfully yanking Franny to her feet. "It's time to go get your trophy."

They took their seats in the auditorium. Nancy Orilee and her parents had moved up to the front row, like guests of honor. The television crew fiddled with their camera on top of the tripod and waited to start filming.

At exactly eight o'clock, the three judges walked up the main aisle and onto the stage. Mr. Pilskog stood at a microphone in the center of the stage. He tapped it twice and cleared his throat until the room fell into silence.

"Before we announce the winners, I'd like to say that whoever walks away with the award tonight, you're all winners," he said.

Yeah, yeah, we've heard that one before, Franny thought rudely. Some of the parents clapped politely, but all of the contestants looked like they knew better.

"And now it's time to announce this year's champion."

Franny leaned forward in her seat, hardly daring to breathe. Lorraine grabbed Franny's right hand and Wes seized her left. The photographers moved to the front of the stage and the TV camera was rolling. Mr. Pilskog cleared his throat again and said: "We judges would like to note that while everyone was very good, one pianist showed particular promise."

Franny smiled, jutting her chin up in the air. She perched on the edge of her seat, ready to spring up the moment her name was called out.

"And the winner is . . . ," announced Mr. Pilskog theatrically, "Nancy Orilee of Rusty Nail!"

The audience let out a collective gasp. All of the contestants looked at each other in shock as Nancy ran up onto the stage. The medal of honor flashed under the spotlights as Mr. Pilskog placed it over her golden head. Cameras flashed as she exclaimed breathlessly, over and over again: "Oh, I knew it, I *knew* it!" She even blew kisses to the audience.

Hot tears filled Franny's eyes and she gulped for breath. How could Nancy have won? *Are those judges deaf?* she thought angrily.

Wes stood up, enraged. "That's outrageous," he said.

"Just outrageous. All I want to know is how much Roger Orilee paid those crooked judges to vote for his spoiled brat of a daughter."

Tears fell down Franny's face once she realized what must have happened. She watched a television reporter shout questions to Nancy.

"What's the secret, Nancy? How'd you get so good?" he asked.

"I'm just a natural, I guess," she said, sweet as sugar. "My daddy always told me that I was the best and there was no way I could lose."

The reporter turned and faced his camera. "Well, folks—that's Nancy Orilee, Minnesota's sweetheart and homegrown piano prodigy."

"Let's go," said Lorraine abruptly, putting her hands on Franny's shoulders and gently steering her into the aisle. Wes collected their things and followed them. Several of the other families had already angrily stalked out.

Olga and Svetlana were waiting in the hallway outside the auditorium.

"*Dyevushka,* you should never cry in front of your audience," Olga said.

"Didn't you see what just happened in there?" shouted Franny, too upset to control herself in front of the Russian. "Nancy was horrible and I was perfect—and she *still* won! It's completely unfair!"

"*Da*—I agree with the girl," said Svetlana. "That Orilee girl was very average and *bourgeois.* It was clear that a bribe happened. I cannot believe that we are seeing such a thing here in America—it is like being home in Russia."

Franny stopped crying out of sheer surprise. She'd never heard the maid make such a long speech before. Usually, she would have been annoyed that Svetlana was butting in, but now she looked at the woman with appreciation.

"Yes, it is very disturbing," Olga said. "I am very sorry, *Dyevushka*. I would not have entered you in this contest if I knew it would be like this. But you should still not cry. A great pianist must always keep her dignity, even in situations like this. No—*especially* in situations like this."

Tears ran down Franny's cheeks again.

"I can't help it," she said. "I'm going to have to go back home and see the whole town celebrating Nancy's big win. It's always the same. Her dad buys her everything she wants: first, she gets fancy piano lessons, then a TV, and *then* first place in the contest! How am I supposed to compete against someone like that?"

"I do not think that the whole town will celebrate Nancy's win," Olga said.

"Why not?" Franny asked.

"Because of the way she won the contest," Olga answered. "There are more people like you in Rusty Nail than people like Nancy and her family. They will side with you, *Dyevushka*—trust me."

"She's right, sweetheart," Wes said. Franny had almost forgotten that her parents were standing there right behind her. Her father bent down and wiped her tears away with his handkerchief. "No one likes to reward a cheater."

"Everyone's just going to think it's sour grapes if we say that they cheated!" Franny cried.

"No, honey—they won't," said Wes. "Roger Orilee has thrown his money around for years, ruling the roost and rigging the system in his favor all the time. The folks at home all know his ways, and they're getting pretty sick of it. No one's going to celebrate the fact that he did it again, especially at the expense of a ten-year-old girl."

This made Franny feel only slightly better. "I just really wanted to win," she said, wiping her face with her sleeve.

"And you *should* have won," Olga said. "But we cannot change the outcome and must find the—how do you say it? The silver line in the cloud."

"Silver lining," Franny said under her breath.

"The important thing is that you have started to compete," Olga went on. "And you have proved that you are an excellent performer."

"Da," piped up Svetlana. "Extraordinary."

What's the point of my being a good performer, thought Franny sullenly, *if you can only win contests with money and not playing well? I'm going to be stuck in Rusty Nail forever.*

Olga was watching her. "I can guess what you are thinking, *Dyevushka,*" she said. "And believe me: bigger things than this contest will come along sooner than you think."

"Like what?" asked Franny.

"Well . . . ," began Olga, gesturing for Svetlana to

come stand next to her. But then, at that moment, Nancy and her family walked out of the auditorium. Mrs. Orilee spotted Olga and trilled out: "Yoo-hoo! Oh, yoo-hoo! Mrs. Koenig! Isn't it just *wonderful*? Our little Nancy—a champion!"

Olga fixed her with a stony stare.

"My name is Madame Malenkov," she said icily.

At this, several newspaper photographers who'd been trailing Nancy looked over and saw the famous Russian. "It *is* Olga Malenkov, fellas!" yelled one of them. "The Commie on the run! Didn't even notice her before now! Get her picture!" They began snapping photos.

Olga ignored them. Instead, she said to Nancy's mother: "Do not bother to send Nancy to my house on Monday."

Then she and Svetlana turned and walked out of the building, with the photographers running along after her.

"Well, I *never*!" gasped Mrs. Orilee. "After all we did for that woman, letting her teach our Nancy! And giving a Commie a chance to be a part of our community." Her eyes narrowed. "It'll be curtains for her now in Rusty Nail."

Lorraine stepped forward. "We'll see about that, Leona," she said. "See you in church tomorrow."

She took Franny's hand, and the Hansens followed Olga out of the building.

Chapter Nineteen

Franny woke up the next morning, back in Rusty Nail and feeling as heavy as an old potato. Still in her pajamas, she trudged into the kitchen.

"Mom, can I stay home from church today?" she asked.

Lorraine didn't even bother to turn around from the counter, where she was slicing bread.

"Not a chance" was her answer. "Be ready to go in an hour."

Dejected, Franny curled up on the living-room couch with a bowl of Wheaties, the so-called Breakfast of Champions, and listened to radio reruns of *Dragnet*.

Suddenly Franny heard footsteps pounding up the stairs to the front door. Without even knocking, Sandy burst into the living room. She wore her Sunday dress and black Mary Jane shoes, an outfit that always looked as amusingly wrong on her as a mink coat sported by a goat.

"I rode my bike into town early to find out what happened at the contest," Sandy said breathlessly.

Tears of humiliation welled in Franny's eyes. "I lost."

"What?" shrieked Sandy. "How? Who won?"

"Nancy did," Franny said. She remembered what Olga had said about not crying and forced her tears back.

"But what *happened*?"

"I'll tell you what happened," Lorraine said, coming in from the kitchen and putting on her church hat. "Nancy's father rigged the contest. It was plain as day. I'm going over to the church early, to have a talk with the mayor and some of the ladies." She looked at Franny. "You can stay and finish your cereal, but you'd better be at church on time for the sermon. And don't forget to drag your father and brothers along with you."

She hurried out the front door.

"I should've known," Sandy said, glowering, helping herself to a bowl of cereal and pouring a huge pyramid of sugar on top. "There's no way that Miss Prissy-priss could've beaten you in a straight contest, and her Daddy Warbucks must've known that all along. Heck—everyone under the sun knows that. Well, Prancy's *not* going to get away with it."

"But she already *did* get away with it," Franny said.

"Even if she cheated and we all know it, she still gets all the fame and glory—and I get nothing. Again."

Sandy opened her mouth to protest but nothing came out. "Yeah," she said, finally. "It's a real tough break." She was quiet for a minute. "And boy, oh boy, is everyone at school who put money in the bettin' pool gonna be mad. Except for one person, who put all of her money on Nancy. And guess who that was?"

"Who?" Franny asked.

"Gretchen Beasley!" Sandy shouted. "It'll be winner-take-all. She's gonna be rich! Who would've guessed it?"

This information only made Franny more miserable. "Just what I need," she said. "To have everyone hate me for losing their allowances to Gretchen Beasley of all people."

"No—*Nancy's* the one they'll be mad at," said Sandy, her mouth full. "Her dad's the one who rigged the contest, not you."

The girls ate their cereal in dismayed silence. Suddenly, something occurred to Franny.

"Hey, Sandy," she said.

"What?"

"How were you planning to pay everyone if I'd won?" she asked.

"Whaddya mean?" asked Sandy.

"You said that the odds were three to one," Franny said. "If I'd won, where would you have gotten the money to pay everyone three times as much as they'd put in?"

Sandy chewed and thought for a minute. "Hmm," she said finally. "Good point. I never thought about that. I just wanted to get your morale up. Maybe it's a good thing you didn't win after all."

She trotted into the kitchen and dumped her bowl into the sink. "Hurry up and get dressed," she called over her shoulder. "For the first time in my life, I wanna get to church on time. I got a feelin' that somethin' big's gonna happen there today."

Franny arrived at church with Sandy, her brothers, and Wes just before the sermon was due to begin. Lorraine sat in the front row, whispering with Mayor Reverend Jerry. Just as the mayor reverend got up to go to his pulpit, the back doors of the church opened and the Orilees arrived with great fanfare. Nancy and Mrs. Orilee wore matching frilly pink dresses and Mr. Orilee grinned at the congregation.

"Sorry we're late," he boomed. "You can start the sermon now that we're here, ha ha."

Mayor Reverend Jerry glared at him. "I'm the mayor, not you, Roger," he said. "God don't look too kindly on folks who exalt themselves and hold up church services for others."

The smile peeled off Mr. Orilee's face as he and his family sat down in an empty pew.

"Now then," Mayor Reverend Jerry said crankily. "Today's sermon's gonna be short, sweet, and to the point."

"That's good news," whispered Wes, who'd woken up too late to have his morning coffee. His hair stuck up in every direction.

"The good book tells us many things," the mayor reverend exclaimed, and opened his Bible. He read out loud: *"For by grace are ye saved through faith; and that not of yourselves: it is the gift of God: not of works, lest any man should boast."*

"What's that supposed to mean?" called out old Hans Zimmerman. "I don't understand a word you jest said."

"*This* is what it means, Hans," thundered Mayor Reverend Jerry, looking right at the Orilees. "It means that the only way to get to heaven is through good deeds. You can't bribe God, the holy judge of us all. And those of us who think they can are in fer a real rude surprise. Bribin's one of the worst sins there is. And folks who don't know that b' now should be spendin' more time with their Bible and less time in the bank. Amen, and dismissed." He slapped his Bible shut and walked off the pulpit.

"Wow," said Wes, looking a little dazed. "I wish that all of his sermons were that short and sweet. Ha—we *told* you that people would root for you, Mozart. Everyone hates a cheater. Now, why don't you go find your mother."

Franny and Sandy scrambled back to the Colosseum,

where they managed to score a few chocolate-glazed doughnuts. All of the women greeted each other and prattled as coffee was handed out.

Then Mrs. Orilee and Nancy swished in, beaming and holding big cardboard boxes.

"Hi, ladies!" sang out Mrs. Orilee. "I got up real early this morning and made cupcakes for everyone! In case you haven't heard yet, our Nancy won the contest yesterday in Minneapolis, and it's time to celebrate! She's in all the papers, and she even got on the TV! Just think: a celebrity right here in Rusty Nail!" Nancy stood next to her mother, a demure look on her face.

Franny expected all of the women to drop everything and rush over to Nancy, cooing their congratulations. But to her surprise, everyone just looked at Nancy and her mother coldly. Lorraine peered into her coffee and smiled faintly.

Mrs. Orilee blinked nervously as she put the cupcake boxes down on the table. "C'mon, girls—don't be shy! One cupcake won't go to your waistline! And I've got something else to say too: I want W.O.R.N.A.T.C.T. to pass a resolution."

Miss Norma Smitty cleared her throat. "All right, Leona," she said. "What is it?"

Mrs. Orilee straightened up. "Well, yesterday, despite all of our good news, we had a very nasty experience with that Commie. In fact, all of our worst fears about her came true. After the contest, out of the blue, she insulted and threatened to harm our Nancy! Can you imagine— threatening a mere child? Now, I'm not only worried about my own little Nancy, but the welfare of every child in Rusty Nail! Is any one of them safe with that vicious Russian spy in town? So, I propose that we go to the mayor reverend and demand that he ban both her and Charlie from the town!"

Franny couldn't believe what she was hearing. "You can't do that!" she yelled, her heart pounding a thousand miles a minute.

"See?" shrieked Mrs. Orilee, pointing at Franny. "She's already tainted one of our youths—what's keeping her from getting her hands on the rest of them?"

Lorraine slammed her cup down on a table. "Now you just shut your mouth right now, Leona," she said. "How *dare* you talk about my daughter that way! And how dare you lie to each and every one of these women about what happened! I was right there yesterday, and Madame Malenkov never, ever threatened your child and you know it. And if you think you're fooling a single person here about why Nancy won that contest, you're dead wrong."

Mrs. Orilee narrowed her eyes and put her hands on her hips. "Ha," she said. "Just try and *prove* it about the contest."

A shocked silence filled the room. This was the single most dramatic thing that had *ever* happened in the

Colosseum, and nearly every woman had her mouth hanging open, especially now that Mrs. Orilee had tacitly admitted to rigging the contest.

"In fact, I'd like to pass a little resolution of my own," Lorraine went on. Franny noticed that her mother's hands were trembling, but Lorraine's voice was as strong and forceful as a flood. "And this is it: I'm starting up another club, and you can't be a part of it unless you renounce membership in the W.O.R.N.A.T.C.T."

Mrs. Charity Engebraten found her voice again. "What new club is that?"

"It's called the W.O.R.N.F.C.S.," Lorraine answered. "And in case you're wondering, it stands for *Women of Rusty Nail for Common Sense*. And its members stand for tolerance and fairness. We'll make pies instead of spreading rumors. Now, who's in? Let's raise hands."

Norma Smitty stood up. "I think that's a real good idea, of course, Lorraine," she said uneasily. "But I don't think we need to go and get rid of the W.O.R.N.A.T.C.T., do—"

"Yes, Norma, I think that we do need to get rid of it," retorted Lorraine. "If there's no Commie threat in Rusty Nail, there's no need for a club like that."

She marched over to her purse and, to Franny's surprise, pulled out the old *Life* magazine Franny had found in Hans's store.

"Just in case any of you need proof, it says right there on page fifty-four that Olga Malenkov is not only *not* a

Commie but is anti-Communist," Lorraine announced, tossing the magazine onto a table in the middle of the room. "In fact, if she went back to Russia, they'd probably kill her. So, girls—you've all been barking up the wrong tree. Next time, Norma, you should do a little homework first."

Mrs. Charity Engebraten snatched up the magazine. Her face got bright red as she read the article about Olga. "Well, I'll be," she said. "Lorraine's right. Don't I feel the fool." She tittered nervously and handed the magazine around.

"I'm staying in the anti-Commie club," scowled Mrs. Orilee, ignoring the magazine even as all of the other women avidly read it.

"Fine with me," said Lorraine tartly. "Bribers, cheaters, and hypocrites need not apply to *my* club. Anyone who supports swindling and lies can just stay in the W.O.R.N.A.T.C.T. Now, all those who're joining the new club, raise your hands."

"Wow," whispered Sandy to Franny. "Don'tcha see what your mother's doin'? She's makin' it so all the women can't stay in the anti-Commie club without lookin' like they're sidin' with Mrs. Orilee! Boy, that's real smart."

She and Franny gaped as women started raising their hands. First, Thelma Britches raised hers, followed by Miss Hamm, who was so far in the back of the room that she was practically glued to the rear wall. Sandy's mother waved her arm. Soon all of the other matrons followed suit. Even Melba raised hers.

"Melba!" said Norma indignantly. "What're you doin'?"

"If you can't beat 'em, join 'em," Melba said lazily. "Who wants t' be left out of a club? And you don't wanna lose business down at the Beauty Station, do ya?"

Norma looked horribly crabby. "No-o," she said. "I guess I don't. But even if I do quit our club and join Lorraine's, that still don't mean that I'm gonna cut and curl that woman's hair. Even if she ain't a real bone-a-fied Commie after all, she's still too uppity for my likin'."

"Do as you please," said Lorraine. "Are you in or out?"

"In, I guess," grumbled Norma. "Can't see that I got a real choice."

Mrs. Orilee slapped the tops down on the cardboard cupcake boxes.

"Fine," she said angrily. "Suit yourselves. But don't come crying to me when your children all go missing, or worse. Have fun with Mrs. High-and-Mighty Hansen over there." With that, she snatched up the boxes and flounced toward the exit. "Come on," she snapped at Nancy, who looked like she was going to cry at any moment.

"Guess there's a new sheriff in town," Sandy whispered to Franny, looking at Lorraine with admiration.

Once the Orilees left, Lorraine let out a deep breath.

"All right," she said, more to herself than anyone else.

"That's over and done with." She walked over to Franny and wrapped her arms around her.

"See, sweetheart?" she whispered to her daughter. "Some things turn out like they're supposed to. Not always, but sometimes. Let's have some crumble cake and go home."

Franny hugged her mother back. This time, she didn't bother to hold her tears back in front of the audience.

Chapter Twenty

Owen was waiting at the door for Lorraine and Franny when they got home from church. He had a funny look on his face.

"What's the matter, sweetheart?" Lorraine asked.

"The Russian lady called here," he said. "She wants Franny to come over this afternoon."

"Why?" Franny asked in alarm. The first thought that flashed in her mind was that Olga was going to drop her because she lost the contest.

"She didn't say," Owen said. "It was real weird to hear her voice. It had an accent and everything, just like in the movies."

"I'm sure it's fine, Franny," Lorraine said, looking weary after the drama at the Colosseum. "She probably just wants to reassure you about the contest. Run along and see her."

Despite her mother's encouragement, Franny still felt nervous when she rang Olga's doorbell. The Russian had never summoned her so abruptly before; in fact, she'd never called Franny's house even once during the whole seven months of lessons.

"Ah, there you are," Olga said, opening the front door. "How was church this morning?"

"You were right," Franny told her. "They all took our side against Nancy and her mom and dad. My mom even started a new club and got Norma Smitty to drop the old one."

"I am glad to hear it," said Olga simply. "And now I have even more news for you. Please sit in the living room. I will be right back." She swept down the hallway toward the kitchen.

Franny walked into the living room, sat stiffly on the edge of one of the settees, and wondered what was about to happen. She had the distinct feeling that Olga was about to disappear from her life for one reason or another, and her heart pounded with anxiety.

Olga marched into the room a minute later with Svetlana in tow.

Franny grew indignant when she realized that the maid would apparently be sitting in, *again*, on her and Olga's personal business.

"Now," Olga said officially as she and Svetlana sat

down across from Franny. "How many years have you been studying the piano, *Dyevushka?*"

"Three or four, I guess," Franny replied. "Maybe more."

"Well," said Olga. "I am sure that you know that I was dead set against teaching you when I first moved here. I was not pleased with the idea of being a teacher to a scrawny small-town girl. I did not think that the arrangement suited a famous concert pianist like myself."

This pronouncement irked Franny, whose ego was already quite bruised from the outcome of the contest.

"So why did you say yes, then, if the idea of teaching someone like me was so horrible?" she asked impudently.

"Because when I heard you play, I realized that you were a special case," Olga answered. "Frankly, your playing sounded like mine when I was your age. It was astonishing."

And then, to Franny's surprise, Svetlana chimed in: "It is a big compliment to say you sound like Olga Malenkov."

This was the last straw for Franny.

"Why is this even your business?" she yelled rudely. "And why are you always sitting in on my lessons? Who *are* you?"

The ladies looked at each other. Finally, Svetlana cleared her throat and said: "I am Madame Svetlana Oblonsky. I was the teacher of Olga at the Juilliard School."

Franny could hardly believe it. Lumpy, coughing, scratching, humming, annoying *Svetlana* was the great master who had taught Olga? Franny wanted to crawl under the sofa from shame.

"Ha—you didn't even suspect, did you, *Dyevushka*?" Olga gloated. "When Svetlana came out to see me here in Rusty Nail, I told her that she must hear my exceptional new protégée. You should know that most pianists would give anything for that opportunity, for the great Svetlana Oblonsky can make or break a career almost overnight.

"Now then," she continued. "I suppose you are wondering why I waited to tell you this about Svetlana, and why we are even having this discussion."

Svetlana looked gravely at Franny and said: "We have decided to offer you a part-time position at the Juilliard School. As part of the pre-college division. I have listened to your playing, and you are very promising. There is no time to be wasted."

Franny's mind suddenly felt as though it was crammed with junk, making it very difficult for her to understand what was happening. "I don't get it," she said.

Olga sighed. "*Dyevushka*—Madame Oblonsky is offering to teach you at Juilliard, in the way that I was taught. So, this would be the appropriate moment to fall on your knees and thank her over and over again."

"You mean, you're saying that I can come study with you all the way out in New York City?" Franny asked, still dumbfounded. "But I live *here*, in Rusty Nail! I'm only ten! What about school? And my parents?" And then she added in a panic: "But I can't cook! How would I *eat*?"

To her chagrin, the women burst out laughing. Seeing how overwrought Franny was, Olga said with uncharacteristic gentleness: "Calm down, *Dyevushka*. There are answers to all of these questions, and they are good answers. You would go to New York this summer, and the next, and the next, and study with Svetlana. It would be like going to camp. And you would go out several times a year, in between summers. Then, when you are old enough, perhaps fourteen or fifteen, you can join the school full-time and start touring.

"But what we are telling you is that the contest on Saturday was *nothing*. You did not know it at the time—but you were not performing for the judges; you were performing for the two of *us*, so we could decide whether your talent was real. And it *is* real. We should know. Going to Juilliard is the way to become a truly excellent pianist. You are being given the opportunity to become a star."

Franny's heart pounded, and she stared at both of them in disbelief. "You're not joking, are you?" she asked. She knew the question sounded horrid, but she knew that she couldn't handle another heartbreak that weekend.

"Of course not," said Olga. "We might be cynical at times—but we are not cruel. You're a natural musician, but now you will have to work very hard—harder than ever before. No more fooling around on pig farms and spying in bushes."

"Wait," Franny said. "You're not going to let Nancy go to Juilliard too, are you?"

Svetlana responded with a *pshaw* sound and waved her hand in dismissal. Olga leaned back in her chair and looked at Franny.

"Nancy is heading for a Miss America contest, not a concert stage," she said. "And why would *we* reward her for what happened in Minneapolis? Her father's money might have bought her that contest, but it cannot buy her the kind of talent it takes to make it at Juilliard and beyond."

"I still don't understand why you agreed to teach her, then, in the first place, if she's so average," Franny said huffily.

"I thought that having your most hated rival competing against you would only make you work harder," said Olga. "And I was right. You accomplished more in several months, striving against her, than you would have in years otherwise."

"How did you know that she was my most hated enemy, though?" Franny asked. "You acted like you didn't even know that we were classmates."

"Charlie told me about the Eunice Grimes concert and how you tried to outplay each other," Olga said. "So, it was perfect. You must, simply *must*, learn how to handle that sort of competition at this age. Believe me, it gets a thousand times more intense later."

Franny thought about leaving her parents and Sandy and Runty, and her stomach sank. "But, Madame Malenkov," she said. "My mother will never let me go. She says it's wrong to give up your childhood to play the piano."

"Oh, you wait and see," said Olga. "I am willing to bet that she will."

Franny suddenly got wildly excited. "I can't believe it!" she shouted over and over again as she leaped off the sofa. Before she realized what she was doing, she threw her arms around Olga. Then she leaned over and hugged Svetlana as well.

"Finally, she shows a little gratitude," Olga said to Svetlana with a sideways little smile. "After all we have done for her. Go home now, *Dyevushka*. I will call your parents and ask them to come here this evening to talk it over."

Franny snatched up her music books, only to drop them all over the floor. On her way out, she almost ran smack into Charlie Koenig, who was just coming home from his trip.

"Whoa there, hotshot," Charlie said, dropping his bags on the floor of the foyer. "Watch where you're going, or you won't like where you end up."

"I *know* where I'm going," shouted Franny joyously. "All the way to New York City!" And she ran down the street toward her house.

All the way home, she saw nothing around her—not the houses on Oak Street, nor the swinging wooden sign above the door of Elmer's Bar, nor the peeling shingles on the front of Hans Zimmerman's store. She didn't see Stella Brunsvold gumming a piece of stale popcorn in front of her stand or a grimy old W.O.R.N.A.T.C.T. flyer lying on the ground near the entrance to the church; nor did she see Melba removing another set of curlers from Mayor Reverend Jerry's hair in the Smitty Beauty Station.

In her mind, Franny was already surrounded by buses and taxis and thousands of people pushing past her on the sidewalks. The quiet streets of Rusty Nail receded as the thundering promise of New York City rushed and crowded into her mind.

That very evening, Franny's shell-shocked parents went to Olga's house and didn't come back until late. Franny had been lying awake for an hour already when they finally walked in. Her brothers snored loudly in their room next door, and she had to strain to listen to her parents' conversation in the kitchen.

"But, Wes," Lorraine said, "Franny's a *child*. She just had her first trip to Minneapolis, for heaven's sake. The idea of sending her to New York every summer on her own is ridiculous. She'll be completely overwhelmed, and besides, it might be dangerous."

"It's not like we'd be sending her on her own, Lorraine," Wes said. "They've been running that program for years, and they really watch the kids closely. And that

Oblonsky woman promised to completely take Franny under her wing."

Lorraine clattered a teakettle heavily on the stove and raised her voice. "Wes—Franny is *not going*!" she yelled. "I'm not sending our baby away, and that's that."

Franny shot up out of bed and scuttled out into the hallway to hear better.

"Lorraine, she's *not* a baby anymore," she heard her father say. "Listen to me. Do you want to be the one to tell her someday that you said no to letting her study with one of the most influential teachers in the world? We didn't ask to have a kid with this kind of talent, but now that we've got her, we have to do right by her."

After a tense silence, Lorraine spoke up. "But how would we afford it?" she asked, her voice wavering. "All of that flying back and forth to New York, and the tuition?"

"Don't worry," said Wes. "We'll find a way. With something this important, we'll just have to."

They dropped their voices and talked for a long time. Unable to hear them anymore, Franny eventually padded back into her bedroom. She crawled into her bed and watched the reflection of the traffic light on the side of the piano.

Yellow, red, green. Yellow, red, green.

She wondered if there would be a traffic light outside her bedroom in New York City.

Epilogue

Two Months Later

Early one Sunday morning, Mayor Reverend Jerry strolled into Hans Zimmerman's store on his way to church. As usual, the old storekeeper sat idly by the cash register, staring into space. Once in a while, he broke his reverie and swatted at a fly with his rolled-up newspaper.

"Dang, Hans," said the mayor. "Don'tcha ever even go home at night? Or do you just set there like a lump on a log twenty-four hours a day?"

"Nah," replied Hans. "I went home last night. Came back real early this mornin'."

The mayor helped himself to some jerky from a jar on the counter. "Is that still the same ole fly?" he asked.

"Who knows," said Hans good-naturedly. "Each one's as good as the last one, and good as the next. What can I get for you, Mayor Reverend?"

"Well," said the mayor grandly. "It's sort of a special day today, and I wanted to bring in some goodies to church for the congregation to celebrate."

"All righty," said Hans. "What's the occasion, and what'd you have in mind?"

"Franny Hansen is leaving for New York City tomorrow," said the mayor. "To study at that fancy music school. I figure that she's as much a celebrity as this town's ever had. So I figured that we should give her a big Rusty Nail bone-voy-age hullabaloo."

"So, you want a cake or somethin'?" asked Hans helpfully.

"Yeah," said Mayor Reverend Jerry. "Show me what you got."

Hans lurched off his chair and shuffled his brittle old frame to the back of the store. He picked up a box of Betty Crocker cake mix and mildly wiped a thin layer of dust off the top.

"Mmm-mm," he said, smacking his lips. "It's lemon flavored."

The mayor frowned. "Now, what am I supposed t' do with a box of mix? I need a whole cake, pronto."

"Wel-l-l," said Hans. "I got a hot plate in the back. You can cook it on that if you want." He looked at the label on the box. "Says here that all we need is a couple-a eggs, some water, and butter. We got all that here. I even got some grease for the pan." He began to walk toward the eggs.

"Now hold it right there," said the mayor. "We ain't even got a pan! And I sure don't have the time to talk good sense into you. Don't you have any cakes that're already cooked?"

The men hunted around the store for a few minutes. The best they could come up with was a couple of boxes of Twinkies, which Hans found behind a stack of hot dog buns.

"That'll have to do," said Mayor Reverend Jerry, looking disappointed. "How much do I owe you?"

Hans creaked back to the cash register and punched a few random buttons. "Thirty-nine cents," he concluded. "So, it's a special occasion, you say? Maybe I should get out the old Christmas lights again."

"That'd be real nice of you," said Mayor Reverend Jerry appreciatively. "It'll get the town in an extra-festive mood again. Remind everyone that Rusty Nail is somethin' special for producin' a young star like Franny Hansen. It's time to leave the American coots behind for good and look to the future."

For the next few minutes, he stood there quietly and thought sentimentally about what he'd just said.

When the mayor left the store, Hans got on all fours

under the front counter and dragged out a worn cardboard box filled with a wild jumble of colored lights.

I sure got my money's worth outta these, he thought. He'd provided the town's electrical goodwill three times in the last twelve months: first with the historical visit of Mrs. Eunice Grimes, then for the months before and after Christmas, and now yet again for the historical departure of Miss Franny Hansen.

"Yessir," he mumbled out loud as he yanked and tugged. "This has been a year to remember."

That same morning, Franny woke up and got ready for church as usual. A typical breakfast scene followed. Lorraine was busy burning the toast when Wes stumbled into the kitchen.

"Lorraine!" he shouted. "What on earth did you do to my church tie?"

Owen and Jessie looked at the tie dangling around their father's neck and burst out laughing. It had shrunken to half its size and was as wrinkled as a prune.

"It looks like a clown tie!" hollered Jessie. "Like a little kid's tie!" Owen doubled over his knees and laughed so hard that no sound came out. Lorraine just shrugged and threw up her hands innocently.

"You got me," she said.

Naturally, the family was late to the sermon. The

whole congregation turned around and looked at them when they came into the church.

Today, unfortunately, Mayor Reverend Jerry's speech was neither short nor sweet. Franny counted sheep while he spoke. But then, at the end of his speech, he said something that caught her attention: "As many of you know, tomorrow Franny Hansen is up and leavin' us for New York City to begin her studies at the Juliet School there."

"*Juilliard* School," hissed some know-it-all from the front pew.

"Yeah, that," said the mayor quickly. "Well, Franny, we want you to know that we're all real proud of you. We'll expect to see your name in the papers and bright lights soon. Don't forget about all of us here in Rusty Nail when you're a big star, y'hear?"

Franny blushed. And then the mayor began to clap, and everyone else joined in: Rodney the jail janitor, mean old Stella Brunsvold, Mr. Klompenhower, old Hans Zimmerman, Miss Hamm, Mrs. Staudt and her ancient father. Even Norma Smitty and Melba clapped a few times.

Wes poked his daughter in the side. "Go on, Mozart," he whispered to her. "Stand up and thank your fans."

With a shy smile, Franny stood up and gave a little bow. When she did this, a loud whoop came from the back of the room. She turned around and saw Sandy and Runty standing on the last pew, stamping and hollering.

And then she noticed that there were three people in

the back of the room who weren't clapping: Mr. Orilee, Mrs. Orilee, and, of course, Nancy, who sat there scowling at the floor. The family had been the town outcasts since the contest in Minneapolis and the showdown between Lorraine and Mrs. Orilee at the Colosseum. Mrs. Orilee remained the sole member of the W.O.R.N.A.T.C.T., while Lorraine's pie-and-common-sense club thrived. Nancy sat alone in the school cafeteria at lunchtime, her nose in the air. And thus, Franny's lifelong and seemingly invincible rival had been vanquished.

"All right, all right," yelled the mayor over the clapping. "That's enough. We don't wanna give Franny a big head. She might not even be able to get through the door of the air-o-plane tomorrow." A few people tittered at this feeble joke and everyone settled down. "Now, let's go get us some refreshments. I got us a treat today, some real gour-mette goodies: Twinkies, Kool-Aid, and coffee in the back. Let's eat."

No one in Rusty Nail *ever* needed to be told twice to eat. Everyone (except the Orilees, of course) stampeded to the Colosseum, where the culinary offerings lay spongily on paper plates.

Franny and her family celebrated with the congregation for the rest of the morning.

Instead of going home with her family after church, Franny walked over to Oak Street to see Olga one last time before her trip. She still worked for the Russian several days a week.

"Have you packed all of your bags, *Dyevushka?*" Olga asked as she opened the front door and ushered Franny inside.

"Not yet," said Franny. "But almost."

"Well, you do not need to pack everything you own, you know," she said. "You are just going for the summer."

"I know," said Franny. "I only have two suitcases." Just then, she noticed a stack of leather suitcases lined up in Olga's foyer. "Wait! Why are *your* bags out? Are you going somewhere too?"

"Yes," said Olga, waving for Franny to come into the living room with her. "I will tell you all about it later this afternoon. But first, I need for you to finish organizing my papers. You are still my indentured servant, you know," she added, and smiled ruefully. Then she went into the kitchen.

Franny had been organizing Olga's personal papers into files for the last month, and only one box remained unopened. Franny cut open the top and saw that it was filled with newspaper and magazine clippings. She took them out and stacked them on the floor, and got ready to organize them by date.

Franny looked at the headline of the first article, dated January 29, 1940, which proclaimed in English:

RUSSIAN VIRTUOSO DEBUTS AT CARNEGIE HALL

She peered at the old black-and-white picture and saw that it was Olga at fifteen or sixteen years old. She quickly thumbed through the rest of the articles.

They were *all* about her teacher—dozens of them, in many languages and strange alphabets—tracking her life and career over the last twenty years. Many of the photos with the articles showed Olga as a young lady playing on various stages, wearing ball gowns. And there she was with the actress Marlene Dietrich; there she was with President Roosevelt. Franny could hardly believe it. Olga always boasted about being a fine pianist, but she had no idea that the Russian was *this* famous.

Then she came across a little pile of articles that looked relatively recent. Sure enough, they had only come out a year earlier, in 1953. The headline on the first proclaimed:

CARNEGIE HALL CANCELS SHOW OF RUSSIAN MASTER

Franny frowned and flipped through the others. Their headlines grew increasingly disturbing:

MALENKOV HEADING FOR THE BLACKLIST?

McCARTHY TO HOLD HEARINGS ON RUSSIAN EXPATS IN NEW YORK CITY

And finally,

INTO THIN AIR—MALENKOV FLEES
NEW YORK CITY

Franny read the first few paragraphs with great interest:

> World-famous pianist Olga Malenkov
> has fled her New York City home and
> is believed to be in hiding, authorities
> said yesterday. Since her debut at Car-
> negie Hall at fifteen years old, Miss
> Malenkov has been considered the fore-
> most performer of Rachmaninoff and
> Prokofiev in the world.
>
> Until recently, she was also con-
> sidered an avid spokesperson against
> the Communist regime in her na-
> tive Russia. However, Senator Joseph
> McCarthy recently announced that he
> was setting up a committee to investi-
> gate the Russian expatriate community
> in New York City.

The article confused Franny, but she read on anyway, hoping to make sense of things. She had the feeling that she was *finally* getting to the root of Olga's secrets: the phone call, the mystery-car incident, the overheard conversation with Svetlana, the references to Rusty Nail being a hideout.

> According to reports, Senator McCarthy wanted Miss Malenkov to testify against several fellow countrymen who were to stand trial. Miss Malenkov reportedly declined his request and shortly afterward left New York. Her lawyer, Charles Koenig of the American Civil Liberties Union, would not disclose his client's whereabouts and declined comment at this time.

Franny's heart leaped. Charles Koenig—wait! That was Charlie!

"Is that very interesting to you, *Dyevushka*?" thundered Olga's voice from the doorway.

Franny jumped and dropped the article. "I was just putting these in order—according to their dates, like you told me to."

Olga picked up the article and looked at it. "So, I guess by now you have solved the big mystery," she said.

"What big mystery?" asked Franny.

"About why I am here in Rusty Nail," said Olga.

★ 262 ★

"I didn't really understand the article," confessed Franny. "But please don't think that I was spying on you again! I just saw it there, and couldn't help reading it! And anyway, I thought that you were here because you married Charlie!"

"It is all right," sighed Olga. "The secret will be out soon enough. In a few weeks, I am going to be in all of the papers and newsreels again."

Franny stood up. "Why—what's going to happen?" she asked.

"What that article was saying, *Dyevushka,* is that I am a *wanted woman,*" said Olga. "The so-called Commie hunter, Senator McCarthy, has set up a hearing in Washington, and in it he wants to prove that many Russians living in New York City are Communists and should get sent back to Russia. He wants me to be his most important witness against these people. But many of them are my friends, who fled Russia when I did—and they are not Communists. If they get sent back there, they will be jailed or worse."

"Then why can't you just get up and tell the truth—that Senator McCarthy is lying about them?" asked Franny.

"I wish that it was that easy," said Olga. "He is a very determined and powerful man. If I try to prove him wrong, he will find a way to punish me. He already has. He had some of my concerts canceled, and could go a lot further. So I ran away, out here, to get away from him and figure out what to do."

Franny suddenly felt a crush of guilt as she remembered the phone call many months ago, when she had accidentally told the caller that Olga lived there. And shortly afterward, the car with the men had shown up.

"Madame Malenkov," she said, tears burning the corners of her eyes. "It's my fault that he found you! I answered the phone when I shouldn't have, and when they asked if you were here, I said yes! And then those men showed up here—it's all my fault!"

"Please stop crying, *Dyevushka*," said Olga. "Remember what I told you about crying when you are supposed to appear strong. I do not want you to think that you are even slightly responsible for what is happening. They would have found me anyway. For all I know, they could have followed my moving truck here. I was only borrowing time, being here."

"What are you going to do?" asked Franny, wiping her eyes.

"Those men who came to the house were delivering a subpoena," explained Olga. "Which means an official notice requiring me to show up at the hearing. So, I must go. In fact, that is why my bags are packed. Tomorrow, I too am flying—to Washington, D.C., where the hearing will take place."

"What are you going to say at the hearing?"

To Franny's shock, Olga's eyes also filled with tears. "I am going to tell them the truth—that my friends are not Communists—and I will bravely face the consequences.

Svetlana came out here to convince me to do this. She reminded me that hiding doesn't make something go away. After all, that is why my parents helped me escape Russia so many years ago—so I could live a free life, not one in hiding like them. It is time to do the right thing and set an example."

She blinked back her tears and took a deep breath. Seeing how upset Franny was, she tried to smile.

"Do not worry about me," she said. "I am sure that I will be fine. After all—what can they do to me? I am the great Olga Malenkov, concert pianist. I have survived much worse things than that sweaty, shouting man. And the tide is turning against McCarthy, slowly but surely. But it will take people like me standing up to him to make that happen."

Franny remembered what Wes had said in the movie theater about the senator: *He'll get his, mark my words.*

"What about Charlie?" Franny asked. "What's he going to do?"

"Charlie is going to come with me," answered Olga. "In fact, here is another big secret, *Dyevushka:* he is my lawyer, not my husband."

Franny almost fell over backward.

"I met him while he was still in law school in New York, many years ago," Olga said. "He was my good friend. When all of the trouble began, I called him, and he has been helping me. He handles cases like this all the time—that is why he is gone on such long work trips.

I do not know who started the rumor about us getting married—probably that Norma Smitty woman—but we decided not to deny it since it would be easier for me to live here in Rusty Nail if everyone thought that we were husband and wife. We knew that the townspeople were going to be scandalized enough by the fact that I was Russian."

"I can't believe it," said Franny, sitting down on the floor amidst all of Olga's articles. "More crazy things have happened since you came to Rusty Nail than ever before."

"Yes, that is probably true," said Olga. "And imagine my surprise, in the middle of this drama, when I came out here to my Rusty Nail hideaway and you turned up on my doorstep. A skinny, determined, and talented pest of a country girl."

Franny's face flushed as she remembered how she'd badgered Olga into giving her lessons, and all of the wangling that had gone into it. Now she realized that the last thing in the *world* Olga had needed was Franny bothering her.

"If I'd known all of that McCarthy stuff was going on, I would've left you alone," she said, embarrassed. "I swear. I'm really sorry."

"Ha!" Olga exclaimed. "I do not believe *that* for a second. You and that friend of yours would have been in that peony bush twenty-four hours a day. Sometimes I still wonder how you managed to talk your way in through the front door and into my music room.

"You know, *Dyevushka,* you are going to have a wonderful future on the stage," the Russian went on, more wistfully now. "And not just because you are such a—how do you say it?—a bacon. You have a wonderful ability to win people over—like you did me."

"Ham," said Franny. "You mean that I'm a ham."

"Yes, that," said Olga. "But also because you loved music and understood it long before you had anyone to truly encourage and guide you. That is the sign of a true gift."

She walked over to the couch and retrieved a little box from behind it.

"I have a little present for you," she said, handing it to Franny. "To remind you of our first meeting, and of your roots here in Rusty Nail, when you are famous and far away."

Franny took the package, which was long and thin and flat. What on earth could it be? Some sort of strange instrument? She zealously tore off the paper and laughed when she saw what lay inside.

The flyswatter.

"Take good care of it." Olga smiled impishly. "I am very fond of it."

Franny picked it up, remembering the night that she and Sandy had camped out in the peony bush, spying. It seemed like a very long time ago, and she felt like a very different person now. She looked at Olga, the person who had changed her life, and tried to think of a way to say how much it all meant to her.

"Thank you" was all she managed, in a squeaky voice.

"You are welcome," said Olga. "Someday you will do the same for another struggling young girl *you* come across. It is like a code of honor with us pianists, despite the competition and jealousy among all of us. After all, the young girl you come across could be the next Mozart or Rachmaninoff, and we all want to advance our art."

Franny nodded solemnly.

"Now finish up your work in here, please," the Russian added, waving toward the stack of articles. "I cannot stand a half-finished job. And I am sure that you want as much time as possible with your family before your life changes forever. And I need time alone before mine does too."

As Olga walked out of the room, Franny heard her say: "I can see your first headline now—*Franny Hansen: Rising Star of Rusty Nail.*"

When Franny left Olga's house and walked home, the stars were coming out, one by one. She stopped and looked at the sky for a long time. It was huge, full of infinity. Tomorrow her teacher would disappear into that sky, off to an unknown future, on to the next tumultuous chapter of an endlessly turbulent life.

Franny had known the Russian for nearly a year, but everything still felt like a dream to her. Somehow, just *somehow*, Olga's life had managed to bump into Franny's and send it in a different direction entirely—like a ball hitting another ball on a pool table and changing its course. It had been an against-all-odds encounter.

But during that time, Franny had learned that this is just how life is: filled with coincidences that later seem like fate. Filled with chance meetings with random people who later become the most important figures in your life. She discovered that success comes from the right person or right opportunity happening to you at the right time in your life.

Of course, she had *sensed* this from the very beginning, which is why she had had the courage to knock on Olga's door in the first place. In this regard, Franny had been wiser than her ten years all along.

But at this moment, she wasn't thinking about any of these things. Instead, she thought about how, the very next day, she would be up there in the sky herself, in an airplane for the first time in her life. She imagined being high up in the blue abyss, surrounded by clouds.

In her mind, she looked back down at the Earth and saw Rusty Nail hundreds of miles below. She could see Main Street and the little brick building where she'd grown up. She saw the crossroads of Oak and Fair streets, where she'd first cut her deal with Olga and become a new person. On the edge of the town, she saw the

Hellickson farm with its streams and cornfields and thick bales of hay. She even thought that she saw Mr. Klompenhower's pig barn.

And then the imaginary plane lifted higher and the land fell away. Franny watched the town disappear altogether. After a moment, she turned her attention to the endless sky above.

Acknowledgments

I would like to express my heartfelt gratitude to the usual suspects: Erin Clarke, my astute editor at Knopf; Christine Earle, my wonderful agent at ICM; Gregory Macek, my stalwart; Caitlin Crounse, my confidante; and Frances J. McCarthy, Esq., my mother and muse.

Lesley M. M. Blume is an author and journalist based in New York City. Her first book, *Cornelia and the Audacious Escapades of the Somerset Sisters,* was released by Knopf in 2006, and was called "a fabulous read that will enchant its audiences with the magic to be found in ordinary life" in a starred review by *School Library Journal.* She is hard at work on her third book.